THOUGHTS OF MURDO

Cover picture by Eric Ritchie

THOUGHTS OF MURDO

IAIN CRICHTON SMITH

BALNAIN

Printed and bound in Great Britain by Cromwell Press
Cover printed by A4 Print
Typeset in Palatino

Published in 1993
by Balnain Books
Druim House, Lochloy Road,
Nairn IV12 5LF
Scotland

The publisher gladly acknowledges the financial assistance of
the Scottish Arts Council in the publication of this volume

British Library Cataloguing in Publication Data
A catalogue record for this book is available from the British
Library

ISBN 1 872557 25 2

CONTENTS

Murdo and the Language

When Murdo went to school at the age of four, he being then about three feet high, a starved-looking very tall thin woman loomed up in front of him.

'You will have to speak English from now on,' she said.

Murdo did not know what to say as he did not know English.

'The cat sat on the mat,' she later told him in confidence.

When Murdo got to learn a little English (there was a direct relationship between his height and the language he spoke) he nearly always spoke it at home, though his mother conversed with him in Gaelic. He would find himself speaking as follows: 'I have much homework to do *an nochd*.' (The explanation for this is that he would start the sentence in English, then remember that his mother preferred Gaelic, and switch to that language. If he had spoken English to his mother she would have called him a snob and no son of hers.)

All this caused Murdo to appear very strange. Thus the reverse might happen at school and he might say, '*Chan eil mo* homework *agam* today.'

A very odd thing happened then. One half of Murdo, vertically visualised, had the colour red: the other half had the colour black. Also it seemed to him that half his tongue spoke Gaelic, the other half English. There was a smell of salt herring from the black half, and a smell of bacon from the other half.

He also at first wrote Gaelic with his right hand and

English with his left hand. Later these physical processes were reversed. In periods of stress he was completely immobilised, i.e he could not write at all. The psychologist who examined him said that he would grow out of all this, after giving him tests about trains, refrigerators, radio stations, and melons, none of which Murdo had ever seen.

When he was at home the colour black pulsed, and when he was in school the colour red glowed.

Sometimes he felt ill in the area of the red, but when he vomited his sickness was black.

As he grew older the red spread over his whole body and there were only little spots of black here and there. Eventually he was all red, and finally the whole skin became a serene white. However, if he was in a company that sang Gaelic songs and emitted torrents of tears, black spots would break out all over his body.

His language too became abstract as he grew older. Thus he might use words such as 'bureaucracy', 'ideology' and 'green belt'. He trained himself not to feel anger or jealousy, for if that happened the black spots reappeared.

People would say to him, 'Och, you are just suffering from the linguistic disease. It will settle down the older you grow. Eventually the black spots will disappear altogether and you will not feel anything at all.' Still he learned and used long words such as 'dichotomy', 'schizophrenic' and 'traumatic'.

Sometimes laughter emanated from him when he remembered that early day on which he had met his teacher and he would recall "The cat sat on the mat". And ever afterwards whenever he saw a cat moving along by a hedge be would think it was in the wrong place.

Neither his handwriting nor his typing ever recovered from this trauma. Part slanted to the right, part to the left. Part (in the case of his typing) was written above the line and part below it.

Such was the linguistic history of Murdo and also why he left the bank, where words like 'draft', 'interest rate', 'bankruptcy,' were used; these words eventually becoming meaningless to him.

NB It is clear from the above that we have here a problem with the narrative "I". For indeed how are we to visualise a narrative "I" which is spoken to in a language that it does not understand. Later, the Narrative "I" is split in two, so that we have two Narrative "I"s, that is Narrative "I"(1) and Narrative "I"(2). No.1 is found at home, No.2 is found in school. Narrative "I"(2) takes over from Narrative "I"(1) and precisely cannibalises it, though not without resentment.

There is a case here for a new kind of criticism which I for the moment as Narrative "I"(3) will not enter into, but which should however be kept in mind for a proper analysis of this phenomenon. (A concept of which Narrative "I"(1) is not aware.)

The colours 'red' and 'black' too are significant. Murdo himself cannot explain this. All we can say is that at times he felt like a traffic light, at other times like a comic. He would have bouts of manic laughter so that both the red and the black would shake. The comical side of him was the red, the tragical side the black. One lip would curl comically red, the other tragically black.

That is all Murdo could say about this linguistic phenomenon.

A Bilingual Poem by Murdo (with Analysis)

Thoir dhomh do lamh, my dearest friend,
is theid sinn a null gu town,
if you'll to me a *sgilling* lend,
neo's math dh'fhaodte a half crown.

Agus ceannaichidh sinne da ice cream,
slider dhut-sa 's dhomh-sa cone,
is ithidh sinn iad ann an dream,
is 'Ta' airson an loan.

Notes:

(1) This is clearly located in Murdo's red and black period.

(2) It can be shown from internal evidence that the black is still quite strong with slight intrusions from the red.

(3) One would suppose that Murdo would be about ten at this point. Also external evidence supports this because of the use of old money, e.g. *'sgilling'*, 'penny', and 'half crown', which is self-explanatory. In addition, the fact that he was eating ice-cream suggest such an age.

(4) Except for someone who speaks English exclusively, the poem is perfectly clear as to meaning.

NB In his poetry readings Murdo was to use his bilingualism as a stylistic device (c.f. Pound and Eliot et Al *).

The only drawback to this was that international audiences on the whole didn't understand Gaelic.

* Al Macleod, an immigrant Canadian poet.

MURDO LEAVES SCHOOL

One day when Murdo was fifteen years old the head-master sent for him.

'Sit down,' he said.

Murdo sat down.

'And what do you intend to do now that you are leaving school?' said the headmaster, who had a small black moustache.

'227 x 67 = 1,809,' said Murdo.

The headmaster looked at him with astonishment and his spectacles nearly fell off his nose.

'Have you any idea at all what you are going to do?' he asked again.

'259 x 43 = 11,137,' said Murdo.

The headmaster then told him that he could leave, that he had much work to do. Murdo saw two girls going into his study with a tray on which there was a cup of tea and two biscuits.

When he came out the other boys asked him what the headmaster had wanted with him and Murdo said that he didn't know.

Anyway, he left the school on a beautiful summer's day while the birds were singing in the sky. He was wearing a white shirt with short sleeves and it was also open at the neck.

When he was going out of the gate he turned and said '45 x 25 = 1,125.'

And after that he walked home.

His mother was hanging clothes on the line and, taking the pegs out of her mouth, she said: 'Your school-days are over: now you will have to get work.'

Murdo admitted that this was true and then went into the house to make tea for himself.

He saw his father working in the field, bent like a shepherd's crook over a spade. Murdo sat at the table and wrote a little verse.

He he said the horse
Ho ho said the goat
Ha ha, O alas,
Said the brown cow in the byre.

He was greatly pleased with this and copied it into a little book. Then he drank his tea.

MURDO LEAVES THE BANK

'I want to see you in my office,' said Mr Maxwell the bank manager, to Murdo. When Murdo entered, Mr Maxwell, with his hands clasped behind his back, was gazing out at the yachts in the bay. He turned round and said, 'Imphm.'

Then he continued, 'Murdo, you are not happy here. I can see that.

'The fact is, your behaviour has been odd. Leaving aside the question of the mask, and the toy gun, there have been other peculiarities. First of all, as I have often told you, your clothes are not suitable. Your kilt is not the attire most suitable for a bank. There have been complaints from other sources as well. Mrs Carruthers objected to your long tirade on the evils of capitalism and the idle rich. Major Shaw said you delivered to him a lecture on Marxism and what you were pleased to call the dialectic.

'Some of your other activities have been odd as well. Why for instance did you put up a notice saying, THIS IS A BANK WHEREON THE WILD THYME BLOWS? And why, when I entrusted you with buying a watch for Mr Gray's retirement did you buy an alarm clock?

'Why did you say to Mrs Harper that it was time the two of you escaped to South America with, I quote, "the takings": and show her what purported to be two air tickets in the name of Olivera? You told her, and I quote, "I'll be the driver while you bring the money out to me. I have arranged everything, even to the matter of disguises."

'You also said, and I quote, "The mild breezes of the Pacific will smoothe away our sin."

'No wonder Mrs Harper left the bank and joined the staff of Woolworths. Other oddnesses of yours can be catalogued, as for instance the advertisement you designed saying, THIS IS THE BANK THAT LIKES TO SAY 'PERHAPS'.

'I have therefore decided, Murdo, that banking is not your forte, and that we have come to the parting of the ways: and this I may say has been confirmed by Head Office. I understand, however, that you are writing a book, and that you have always intended to be an author. We cannot, however, have such odd behaviour in an institution such as this. Imphm.

'Also, you phoned Mrs Carruthers to tell her that her investments were in imminent danger because of a war in Ecuador but that you were quite willing to fly out for a fortnight to act as her agent. When she asked you who you were, you said, "Mr Maxwell, and his ilk."

'You also suggested that an eye should be kept on Mr Gray as, in your opinion, he was going blind, but he was too proud to tell the bank owing to his sense of loyalty and to his fear that he might lose his job, as he was supporting three grandchildren. Such a man deserved more than money, you said, he required respect, even veneration.

'You have in fact been a disruptive influence on this office, with your various-coloured suits, your balloons, and your random bursting into song.

'Have you anything to say for yourself?'

'It is true,' said Murdo, after a long pause, 'that I have been writing a book, which I shall continue after I have suffered your brutal action of dismissal. It will be about the work of a clerk in a bank, and how he fought for Blake's grain of sand against watches and umbrellas. Banks, in my opinion, should be havens of joy and pulsing realities. That is why I have introduced fictions, balloons, masks, toy guns, and songs.

'You yourself, if I may say so, have become to my sorrow little better than an automaton. I do not advert to your sex life, and to your obsession with yachts, but I do advert to the gravestone of your countenance, to your strangled "Imphm", and to your waistcoat. Was this, I ask myself, what you always wanted to be, when you were playing as a young child at sand castles? Is this the denouement of your open, childish, innocent face? Why is there no tragedy in your life, no comedy, no, even melodrama? You have hidden behind a mound of silver, behind a black dog and a Nissan Micra. Regard yourself, are you the result of your own dreams? What would Dostoevsky think of you, or Nietzche? Are the stars meaningless to you, the common joys and sorrows? You may pretend otherwise, Mr Maxwell, but you have lost the simple clownish heart of the child. Nor indeed does Mrs Maxwell have it as far as my observations go. I leave you with this prophecy. There will come a day when the vault will fail and the banknote subside. The horses of hilarity will leap over the counter and the leopards of dishevelment will change their spots. The waves will pour over the cravat and the bank that I have labelled 'Perhaps' will be swallowed by the indubitable sands of fatuity. What price your dog then, your debits, and your accounts? What price your percentages in the new avalanche of persiflage? In the day when the giant will overturn the House of the Seven Birches what will you do except crumble to the dust? Nor shall there be special offers in those days, and the brochures will be silent. Additions and subtraction will fail, and divisions will not be feeling so good. Computers will collapse, and customers will cast off their chains. Cravats will cease and crevasses will no longer be concealed.'

In a stunned silence, he rose and said, 'That is my last word to you, Mr Maxwell, and may God protect you in his infinite mercy.'

He pulled the door behind him and walked in a dignified manner to the street, in his impeccable red kilt and hat with the red feather in it.

Murdo's Letter to the Poet Dante

Dear Friend,

Can you please tell me when and how you first began to write, and what magazines you sent your first poems to? And what was the animal you saw in the middle of the wood?

For myself, I see this white mountain all the time, day and night. With snow on it.

And in the room next to me there is a table and chairs as like each other as pictures in a mirror. Anyway, I hope you will answer my letter for I am trying to write a story about a clerk.

And I don't know how to start.

With much respect and a stamp so that you can answer my letter.

Yours sincerely,
Murdo Macrae

P.S. You did very well, my friend, with that poem the INFERNO. But what would you have done without Virgil? I think we all need a friend.

Murdo Meets Mrs Macleod

One morning Murdo put on a red rubber nose such as clowns wear, or small children at Halloween, and went down town to get the morning papers. Norman Macleod's wife met him at the door of the shop and he said to her: 'It's a fine morning.'

'Yes,' said she, looking at him slightly askance, since he was wearing a red rubber nose.

'But it is not as beautiful a morning as it was yesterday,' Murdo said seriously. 'Not at all as good as yesterday morning. No indeed.'

'You're right there,' said Norman Macleod's wife, looking at his nose. Murdo pretended that he didn't notice her amazed stare.

'You're right there indeed,' said Murdo. 'I myself am of the opinion that it is not so warm this morning as it was yesterday morning,' glancing at the snow that glittered back at him from the roadside.

'Without doubt, without doubt,' said the wife of Norman Macleod.

'For,' Murdo pursued relentlessly, 'the clouds were whiter yesterday than they are today,' drawing nearer to Mrs Macleod and putting his red rubber nose quite close to her face.

'For,' said Murdo, 'when I got up from my bed this morning I nearly went back into it again, a thing that I did not think of doing yesterday. But in spite of that I put one leg in front of the other as we all have to do in this life at some time or other, indeed at all times, and I decided that I would come for the newspapers, for what can we do without them? What indeed?'

'You're right,' said Mrs Macleod, shifting slightly away from him.

'Yes,' said Murdo, 'in these days especially one must put one leg in front of the other. When the light comes out of the darkness we go in search of the DAILY RECORD, those sublime pages that tell us about the murders that have been committed in caravans in the south.'

'Yes,' said Mrs Macleod in a voice that was becoming more and more inaudible as she moved further and further away from the red rubber nose.

'I myself often think,' said Murdo, 'how uninteresting my life would be without the DAILY RECORD. That occurs to me often. Often. And often I think what would we do without neighbours? Their warmth, their love.... These thoughts often occur to me, I may tell you.'

'I suppose...' muttered Mrs Macleod, her grip tightening on the newspaper she had in her hand as if she was thinking of using it as a weapon.

'For,' said Murdo intently, 'do you yourself not think that the warmth of the morning is like the warmth we derive from our neighbours. The sun shines on everything and so does the warmth of our neighbours? There is a lot wrong with each one of us, we are all flawed in some way, but our neighbours forgive us for they say to themselves, "Not one of us is perfect, not one of us is without flaw, so how therefore can we say that others are flawed." These are the thoughts that often occur to me anyway,' said Murdo. 'And I don't think I'm wrong.'

'I'm sure you're...', said Mrs Macleod, trying to back steadily away while Murdo fixed her closely with his red rubber nose as if he were a demented seagull standing among the snow.

'Give me,' said Murdo, 'one neighbour and I will move the world.' He considered this for a long time, turning his nose this way and that, the only bright colour that was to be seen on the street. Mrs Macleod wanted desperately to leave but she couldn't move her feet, and she didn't know what to say.

Murdo went closer to her.

'I am of the opinion,' he said, 'to tell the truth and without concealing anything from any man or woman, white or black, whoever they are and whatever their colour of skin, I am of the opinion without regard to anyone's politics or religion, for no one can accuse me of being biased, that yesterday morning was as beautiful a morning as we have had for many years. I'm not saying that there don't exist people who would deny that, and who would come to me if they liked with armfuls of records going back to the seventeenth century and before, that would prove that I was wrong, and even naive in that statement, but in spite of that I still hold to my opinion, as I am sure you would under the same circumstances, for I have never thought of you as a coward. Oh, I know that there are people that will maintain that neither the summers nor the winters that we endure now are as beautiful and unspotted as the summers and the winters of their various childhoods, but I would say humbly to these people that they are wrong. THEY ARE WRONG,' he shouted, pushing his nose as close to Mrs Macleod's nose as it would go.

'THEY ARE WRONG,' he repeated in a loud vehement voice. 'As wrong as people can be. I know in my bones that they are wrong. Totally wrong. Totally.' He sighed heavily and then continued: 'As well as that I know that there are professors who would oppose me in this matter. But I know that they are wrong as well. Though I have nothing against professors. Not at all, not at all.

'But I'm keeping you back. I shouldn't have done that. I know that you're busy, that you work without cease, without cease. Lack of consideration, that's what I suffer from. I admit it freely. But I wished to tell you how much more beautiful than this morning yesterday morning was. And I'm glad that you agree with me in my opinion. I am so glad. So glad. It is not often that I feel such gladness. But I know that you wish to go home. I am so glad to have met you.'

Mrs Macleod half walked, half ran, away, looking behind her now and then as if trying to verify that he did indeed have a red rubber nose. Murdo raised his hand to her in royal salute and then went into the shop, having first removed his rubber nose, and bought a newspaper. On his way home he would kick a lump of ice now and again with his boot.

'Drama,' he said to himself. 'Nothing but drama and catharsis. One must look for it even when there is snow on the ground.'

He arrived at a wall and opened out the paper and began to read it, glancing now and again at the white mountain.

He read one page and then threw the paper away from him, but after a while he picked it up and laid it flat on a large piece of ice.

The headlines of the paper said in large black type:

> **I STILL LOVE HIM**
> **THOUGH HE KILLED FOR ME**

Murdo found an old boot in the ditch and laid it on top of this headline so that passers-by could read it, and then went whistling on his way.

MURDO'S ADVERTISEMENT

This is an advertisement which Murdo sent to the editor of the local paper but which was never printed.

> **WANTED:**
> A man of between a hundred
> and two hundred years of age
> who knows the work of Kant and
> the poetry of
> William Ross,
> and who can drive a tractor
> and a car,
> for work on the roads for three
> weeks in the year.
> Such a man will get
> — particularly if he is healthy —
> two pounds a year.
> It would be an advantage if he
> knew a little Greek.

MURDO & HIS MOTHER-IN-LAW

Sometimes, when they were sitting in the kitchen Murdo would come over to his wife with a piece of paper on which he had written some such word as BLOWDY.

'What do you think that word means?' Murdo would say to her.

'Blowdy?' Janet would say. 'I never heard that word before.'

'Didn't you?' Murdo would say. 'Blowdy,' he would say to himself again. 'Blowdy, blowdy,' among the chairs, the green walls.

Once, when his mother-in-law was in drinking tea, Murdo said to her quietly: 'It's a fine blowdy day today.'

'What did you say?' said his mother-in-law, the cup of tea in her lap and a crumb of bread on her lip.

'A fine blowdy day,' said Murdo, 'a fine windy, bright, blowdy day.'

'It's a windy day right enough,' said his mother-in-law, looking meaningfully at Janet.

'That's an Irish word,' said Murdo. 'The Irish people used it to give an idea of the kind of marbly clouds that you sometimes see in the sky on a windy day, and also when the wind is from the east.'

'Oh?' said his mother-in-law, looking at him carefully. When Murdo had gone back to his room she said to

Janet: 'I don't think Murdo is all there. Do you think he is?'

'Well,' said Janet, 'he acts very funny at times.'

'He's worse than funny,' said her mother. 'Do you remember at the wedding when he took a paper ring from his pocket and he was wearing a piece of cabbage instead of a flower like everybody else?'

'I remember it well enough,' said her daughter. 'But he is very good at figures.'

'That's right enough,' said her mother, 'but a man should be more settled than he is. He should be indeed.'

After her mother had left, Janet sat in the chair and began to laugh and she could hardly stop, but at the same time she felt frightened as if there was some strange unnatural being in the house with her.

MURDO'S LETTER TO THE PRIME MINISTER

Sir—

I am of the opinion that there is a strong conspiracy afoot to undermine this country of ours.

Why do people sit watching TV all the time? I am convinced that there are certain rays that come out of the TV set and that these rays are causing people to lose their commitment to the pure things of life.

Did you ever consider the possibility that John Baird was a Communist?

Do you really believe that there is no connection between the rise of TV and the rise of Communism in the Western world?

Who controls TV? Let me ask you that. Let me put that question to you in all sincerity.

An if the Russians attack this country what would our people be doing? I think they would continue to sit and watch the TV.

AND THEY WOULD NOT BELIEVE IT WAS AN ATTACK BY THE RUSSIANS AT ALL. THEY WOULD THINK IT WAS A TV DOCUMENTARY.

Did that ever occur to you?

And as well as that there are many people who do not believe that you yourself exist at all. They believe that you have been assembled on TV. If this is false please answer at once and establish your identity.

With great respect,

Murdo Macrae

I nearly signed my letter PRO PUBLICO BONO but there has been such a decline in the Latin language that I could not do so. And what is the cause of that? Is it not the TV?

MURDO IN THE LIBRARY

One day Murdo visited the local library and he said to the thin bespectacled woman who was standing at the counter: 'I want the novel WAR AND PEACE written by Hugh MacLeod.'

'Hugh MacLeod,' she said.

'Yes,' he said, 'but if you don't happen to have WAR AND PEACE I'll take any other book by the same author, such as THE BROTHERS KARAMOZOV.'

'I thought,' she said doubtfully, 'I mean, are you sure that...'

'I am quite sure that the book is by Hugh MacLeod,' said Murdo, 'and I often wonder why there aren't more of his books in the libraries.'

'Well,' she said, 'I think we have WAR AND PEACE but surely it was written by Tolstoy...'

'What's it about?' said Murdo. 'Is it about a family growing up in Harris at the time of Napoleon?'

'I thought,' she said, 'that the story was set in Russia,' looking at him keenly through her glasses.

'Bloody hell,' said Murdo under his breath, and then aloud, 'Oh, well, I don't think we can be talking about the same Hugh MacLeod. This man was never in Russia as far as I know. Is it a long book, about a thousand pages?'

'I think that's right,' said the woman, who was beginning to look rather wary.

'Uh, huh,' said Murdo. 'This is a long book as well. It's about Napoleon in Harris in the eighteenth century. Hugh MacLeod was an extraordinary man, you know. He had a long beard and he used to make his own shoes. A strange man. I don't really know much about his life except that he became a bit religious in his old age. but it doesn't matter. If you haven't got WAR AND PEACE maybe you could give me his other book THE BROTHERS KARAMAZOV. It's about three brothers and their struggle for a croft.'

'I don't think,' said the woman, 'that we have that one.'

'Well, isn't that damnable,' said Murdo. 'Here you have an author as distinguished as any that has ever come out of the Highlands and you don't have his books. And I can't get them in any other library. I think it's shameful. But I bet you if he was a Russian you would have all his books. I'm pretty sure that you will have TRAMPING THROUGH SIBERIA by Gogol. Anyway, it doesn't matter.

'But I was forgetting another reason for my call,' and he took a can out of his pocket. 'I'm collecting money for authors who can't write. A penny or two will do.'

'Authors who can't write?' said the woman, looking suspiciously at the can as if it might explode in her face.

'That's right,' said Murdo, 'poor people who sit at their desks every morning and find that they can't put a word to paper. Have you ever spared a thought for them? Those people who can write don't of course need help. But think,' he said, leaning forward, 'of those people who sit at their desks day after day, while the sun rises and the sun sets, and when they look at their paper they find that there isn't a word written on it. Do you not feel compassion for them? Aren't your bowels moved with pity? Doesn't it surprise you that in our modern society not enough is done for such people?'

'Well,' she said, 'to tell the truth...'

'Oh, I know what you're going to say,' said Murdo. 'Why should you give money for non-existent books? And that point of view is natural enough. There is a great deal in it. But has it ever occurred to you that the books that have never been written may be as good as, nay even better than, the ones that have? That there are in some heaven or other books as spotless as the angels themselves without a stain of ink on them? For myself, I can believe this quite easily as I put a lot of credence in the soul, as I am sure you do also. Think,' he said, 'if this room were filled with non-existent unwritten books how much easier your job would be.'

He saw her hand creeping steadily towards the phone that lay on her desk and said hurriedly, 'Perhaps that day will come, though it hasn't come yet.'

He took the can in his hand and half walked, half ran, out of the library down the corridor with the white marble busts of Romans on each side of him.

Still half running he passed a woman laden with books, and said, 'I'm sorry. Bubonic plague. Please excuse me. I'll be all right in a few minutes. Brucellosis,' and half crouching he ran down the brae among the bare trees and the snow.

Ahead of him he saw the white mountain and he shook his fist at it, shouting, 'Lilian Beckwith, Lilian Beckwith.'

After a while he took a black hat out of his bag and went home limping, now and again removing his hat when he saw a child walking past him on the street.

MURDO AND THE POTATO

'The potato,' said Murdo to his wife one night, 'what would we do without the potato? What would we do without the potato especially in the islands? The potato is sometimes wet and sometimes dry. It is even said that the dry potato is "laughing" at you. Now that is a very odd thing, a laughing potato. But it could happen. And there are many people whose faces are like potatoes. If we had no potatoes we would have to eat the herring with our tea and that wouldn't be very tasty. In the spring we plant the potatoes and we pick them in the autumn. Now, in spite of that, no poet has made a poem for the humble potato. It didn't occur to William Ross or Alexander MacDonald — great poets though they were — to do so, and I'm sure they must have eaten a lot of potatoes in their poetic careers.

'There is a very big difference, when you think of it, between the potato and the herring. The herring moves; it travels from place to place in the ocean, and they say that there aren't many fish in the sea faster than the herring. But the potato lives in the dark until someone digs it up with a graip. We should therefore ask ourselves, which is the happier of the two, the potato or the herring? That is a big philosophical question and it astonishes me that it hasn't been studied in greater depth. It is a very profound question. For the potato lives there in the dark, and it doesn't hear or see anything. But in spite of that we have no evidence that it is less happy than the herring. No indeed. And as well as that we have no evidence that the herring is either happy or unhappy. The herring journeys through the ocean meeting many other kinds of fish on its way, such as seals and mackerel. But the potato stays in the one place in the dark in its brown skin, without, we imagine, desire or hope. For what could a potato hope for? Or what could it desire? Now at a certain time, the potato and the herring come together on the one plate, say, on a summer day or even an autumn day. It greatly puzzles me how they come together in that fashion. Was it predestined that that particular herring and that particular potato should meet — the herring that was roving the sea in its grey dress and the potato that was lying in the earth in its brown dress? That is a very deep question. And the herring cannot do without the potato, nor for that matter can the potato do without the herring. For they need each other.

'They are as closely related as the soul and the body. But is the herring the body or the soul?

'That is another profound question.

'And also you can roast a potato and you can roast a herring, but I don't think they are as good when they are roasted. I myself think that the herring is better when it is salted, and I may say the same about the potato.

'But no one has ever conjectured about the feelings of the potato or the feelings of the herring. The herring leaves its house and travels all over the world and it sees strange sights in the sea, but the potato sees nothing; it is lying in the darkness while the days and the weeks and the years pass. The potato doesn't move from the place where it was planted.

'I must make a poem about that sometime,' said Murdo to his wife. 'I am very surprised that up till now no one has made a poem about it.' And he stopped speaking and his wife got up and made some tea.

MURDO
and
CALVIN

One day Murdo went into the police station.

'I wish,' he said, 'to report something.'

'And what is that, sir?' said the sergeant, who was large, polite, and red-faced.

'I wish to report,' said Murdo feverishly, 'a sighting of Calvin.'

He paused impressively.

'And which Calvin is that, sir?' said the sergeant quietly. 'And why should you report him?'

'Calvin, Sergeant, is a dangerous lunatic. He is responsible for the Free Church, for the state of Scottish literature, and for many other atrocities too numerous to mention. And especially the Kailyard,' he added in a low voice.

'Kailyard, sir?'

'That's right, Sergeant. One of his grossest inventions. I want him arrested.'

'But, sir,' said the sergeant, 'I can't ...'

'I haven't finished yet,' said Murdo in a penetrating voice. 'I believe him also to have committed the greatest sin of all. I can only tell you in a whisper. I believe him to have invented the Bible.'

'Invented the Bible, sir?'

'That's right, sergeant. I have always suspected that the Bible was the invention of one man, a man with a colossal ego and a criminal mind. Let me ask you this. If the Bible had been invented by God would it contain all the mistakes that it contains. For instance,' he said rapidly, 'how is it that God is supposed to have created light before making the sun or the moon? You can read of that error in Genesis. That is only one example. Another example is this. What woman was supposed to have married Cain when there was no other woman alive on the face of the deep but his own mother Eve? They suggest to me the inventions of a man who was not naturally creative and, as we know, Calvin — like Francis Bacon, another treacherous man — was a lawyer.

'Listen, in the Bible there's a man called Amraphel, one called Ashteroth, and another one called Chedorlaomer. There are the names invented by a tired mind. Also, he made other slips in this gigantic enterprise. He said that Reu lived after he begat Serug two hundred and seven years. All this suggests a man engaged in the creation of a stupendous best-seller whose mind flickered at the typewriter. Have you any idea, Sergeant, how many copies of this vast book have been sold in the last thousand years? It is the most bizarre plot in human history.'

'But, sir, I...' the sergeant tried to intervene.

'And that is not all by any means,' said Murdo, his eyes assuming a supernatural sharpness and directness. 'If you will allow me to continue. There is also this fact which I think is almost conclusive. A book of such magnitude must have taxed even the greatest brain. And so we find whole chapters which are feverish outpourings making no sense at all, either that or these are space fillers pure and simple. How else can one explain whole chapters which run as follows?

'And Shem lived after he begat Arphaxad five hundred years, and Arphaxad lived three and thirty years and begat Salah, and Arphaxad lived after he begat Salah four hundred and three years. And this, mark you, Sergeant, is the lowest limit of some of the ages. Think, Sergeant, of the huge amounts of money that would have to be paid in old age pensions if that were true. Think of the drain on the Health Service, the hospitals required, the Social Security, the guide dogs, the food, the drink, the white sticks, the geriatric wards. How could any economy have sustained such a vast number of the ancient, especially before television was invented. Look, sergeant, it cannot be denied that there is at least here a basis for investigation.'

The sergeant's round reddish eyes gazed at him.

'All the oxen and the asses,' continued Murdo relentlessly, 'that one could covet. Is there not something there too? Crimes unimaginable. A fiction of such remarkable cunning that it is difficult for us to understand the ramifications of its plot. The sex, the murders, the casual examples of incest, sodomy, black magic and theft. The silences on important matters like justice and religion. It has been clear to me for many years that at the back of all this was Calvin. Tell me this,' said Murdo earnestly, 'if you were going to investigate a criminal would you not ask yourself certain questions? Ah, I see that you would. Who, you ask, gains by such an immense crime. And you must answer if you look around your country today that the only person to gain must be Calvin. Wasn't it he and his church who became triumphant? Who therefore would be more likely to bring such a result about? Ah, you are now going to ask me the most penetrating question. Opportunity. Did Calvin in fact have the opportunity? You may say reasonably enough that Calvin lived centuries ago but was not so old as the Bible. That puzzled me for a while too, till eventually I saw the solution to it. And I found the solution, as commonly happens, in his own work. You remember that he mentioned a number of people who lived to the age of eight hundred. I believe that Calvin lived to the almost unimaginable age of 22,000 years five months and two days. He waited and waited, keeping his manuscript intact, till one day the printing press was invented and he pounced (is it a coincidence by the way that Calvin differs from Caxton by only three letters?).

'I can tell you, sergeant, that on that day Calvin was in his element. Imagine what it must have been like for him to know that his book, once a scroll, would be read all over the world, that boats would ferry his best-seller to the ignorant Africans, Asians and the Scots. Imagine the size of the royalties.

'And now he is here and I have seen him. He will hardly leave his house (for his cunning is supernatural) and I only saw him briefly while he was completing his toilet on the moor. He will speak to no women and if any come near him he will shake his stick at them and mutter words like, "Impudent whores, prostitutes of the deepest dye." And that is another thing,' said Murdo vigorously, boring his eyes towards the crab-red eyes of the sergeant. 'A writer can be told by his convictions, by his mannerisms. Calvin hated women and this appears in the Bible. In nearly every case the women are either treacherous or boring. He hated sheep as well: think of the number that he sacrificed. Who is this man then, this woman-hater, this sheep-hater-genius who has deceived so many million people, ambitious inventor of strange names? What other evidence do you need?'

He stopped and the silence lasted for a long time.

'But I have not,' Murdo continued, 'reached the highest point of my deductions yet. It came to me as a bolt from the blue as bolts often do. The beauty of it is breathtaking. Let me list those things again: a man who hates women, who deceives men, who lives thousands of years, who will stop at nothing for gain, who has come out of hiding at this present disturbed time, who wears a bowler hat, whose sense of humour is so impenetrable that no one can understand it, who imposes such colossal boredom on the world that no one can stay awake in his presence, a man who uses boredom as a weapon. Who, I repeat, is this man? I will tell you,' and he lowered his voice again. 'I believe that this man is the Devil.' He leaned back in triumph. 'There, I have said it. Think how many problems that solves at a stroke. Think how the knots untie themselves, if we once understand that Calvin is the Devil. Everything that was opaque to us before is now crystal clear. All the questions that we need to ask are answered. You must,' he said decisively, 'send a Black Maria for him at once, or a green one or even a blue one, before he can start on more books of such length. Is he planning to come out of hiding to demand his royalties? Think of our country. How could it withstand such a demand? Surely you of all people can see that... Ah, I understand, you aren't going to do anything. I was afraid of that. Well, don't say that I didn't warn you when the consequences of his arrival here become clear.' He backed towards the door, the sergeant leaning across the desk towards him. 'Remember that I warned you. You have my phone number, my fingerprints. I have nothing to gain. We know who has something to gain.' He screamed as he went round the door. 'Put him in a cell or he'll destroy us all. Bring him in on suspicion of loitering, of parking on a double yellow line, of singing at the Mod.'

The sergeant strode towards the door and locked and bolted it. He was breathing heavily. And even yet he thought that he could hear that voice shouting, '... for being a hit man for the Educational Institute of Scotland.'

Murdo's
Manifesto for the Council

Leaving aside a long philosophical disquisition in which I had hoped to include remarks from Kafka, Dostoevsky, Sartre and others, I will advert to the matter at hand.

Drain Pipes: These are clearly inadequate and should be replaced. I have not the technical knowledge to discuss this matter in much detail, though I am sure my opponents will speak as if they were engineers, sewage repairers, etc. I will begin as I have started, wielding a broad brush and leaving the details to lesser more bureaucratic minds who have degrees in Drain Pipes, etc.

For myself, I will stick to authentic anecdotes for the People, without whom this election would be meaningless. It is for them that we are fighting, and we must not forget that, and no blurring of questions by those who pretend to be sewage engineers will blind them to what is happening. Suffice it to say that the whole system of Drain Pipes will have to be replaced and kept constantly in review. I accuse Councillor Macleod of gross neglect in this area and though I know his family well I call on him to resign.

Education: This is a subject on which I am willing to speak at length, and with expertise. Here I wish to make more provocative statements in order to waken up the docile island proletariat. I accuse our education masters (dim shapes indeed) of having created competent soulless people. Where is the imagination? Where are our ideas of angels and demons, where are our dreams, our visions? What use to us is spelling, the numbers table, history, geography, etc? These lead us to become like Mr Maxwell, the bank manager, and his tombstone visage. We need visages more radiant than that if we are to survive spiritually, economically, etc.

With regard to **Geography**, why do we need to know the location of Hong Kong, Rangoon, Canberra, etc? The Norsemen, the Picts, the Anglo Saxons, did not know of them. Did this prevent them from leading happy contented and, on the whole, ravaging lives? What would it have availed a Pict to know of Sumatra or for an Anglo Saxon to be apprised of Tasmania? That will suffice, I think, for Geography.

With regard to **History**, what is Richard II to me or I to Richard II? Were I ignorant of the Battle of Thermopylae, or of Charlemagne, would this disturb my nights? Can Henry VIII help me with my existential decisions, or Boadicea heal me of my wounds? Can Edward I help me to take the mote out of my neighbour's eye? So much for History.

No, Education prevents the unfettered use of the Imagination. It hampers us with facts, and torments us with dates. It confuses us with ideologies, and delays our progress towards the infinite. Read Blake, read Lawrence, but not Plato who kept the poets out of his Republic.

Sailings: I am totally against sailings on weekdays and would confine them to Sundays, for it is on that day that we are most at ease and can take advantage of perfumed breezes, clear skies, etc. On weekdays, burdened as we are with material thoughts and economic notions, we cannot take advantage of the innocence of the sea, and its sinless expanse.

Toilets: My opponents say that there are too few toilets available: I say, on the contrary, that there are too many. Too many toilets, even one toilet, leads to drugs, graffiti, conspiracies. Every right-thinking person has a toilet in his own house: why does he need more? Before going on a journey he should make a habit of using the toilet. If, however, he is as they say "caught short" he should knock on someone's door and ask if he can use their toilet. This would go a long way to maintaining friendship and the community spirit and the oral tradition.

Bridges: These should be eliminated. People should as much as possible stay in their own village. Only the unimaginative travel. As Pascal said, Much of the trouble in this world is caused by people who won't stay in their own rooms. If people are confined to their own villages they will use their imagination more and will be constrained from talking about wars, space shots, etc. Lisbon, Madrid, Rome, these are matters for our dreams, and the reality of Venice is never as beautiful as the Venice of our imagination.

Hospitals: There should be fewer wards, fewer nurses, fewer doctors. Most illnesses are caused by other people's minds: these are the true sources of infections. Boredom has much to answer for, as indeed have envy, spleen, jealousy and hate. For myself I am free of all these emotions, though I am not sure that my opponents are. Let the bacilli of rancour flourish elsewhere: hospitals are where they breed most. If we had no hospitals, who would have thought of them? If we had no Anadin, who would have invented it. Doctors are vampires on our emotions: they make money from our hatreds. Nurses will miss their watches and their thermometers and indeed their power, but they can be given other paraphernalia. Bedpans will vanish from the landscape; there will be less demand for grapes; lucozade will be no more. Visiting hours will no longer exist, and waxed floors will disappear. Death will die, as it will no longer have the oxygen of publicity.

Finally, though I do not wish to personalise my **Opponents**, there are a few facts that you should know about them.

Mr Chevenix Trench, my Tory opponent, has worked for the Post Office for more years than I can care to count. His horizons therefore are limited to stamps, postal orders and registered parcels. What does he know of foreign policy who foreign policy does not know? Ask him what the capital of Afghanistan is. Will he know it? I think not. He has had no need to examine his life, which is now a struggle for naked power. He works from nine to five every day. What does he do with the rest of his time? I suggest to you that his mind cannot rise above letter-boxes and that his imagination is confined to telephone bills. Touch him, and he gives out a tinkle of nullity. Avoid him, do not be deceived by his busy air of vacuity. You are too intelligent to be taken in by such a nefarious mystagogue. Let him take his ambition elsewhere. In any case he has been involved in a messy divorce.

With regard to my SDP opponent, Mr R Green, what can I say of him? Where are his policies, his intuitions, his imagination? He arrived here first as a photographer, then became a hotelier. His photography was bad, his food is worse. His red banal face, his hail-fellow-well-met attitude are a front for the deepest emptiness. Feel his hand, it is wet with soup and false bonhomie. Look him in the eye: he is thinking of his tariff. He has patronised you by learning a few words of Gaelic. However, if you ask him what the Gaelic for "werewolf" is, he does not know. Nor indeed the Gaelic for "bonhomie". What is his position on the ozone layer? He does not know. Or the green house effect? He has never heard of it. Or the Indeterminacy Principle: his animadversions on that would be laughable.

NO, VOTE FOR ME, YOUR COUNCILLOR WHO CAN DELIVER, WHOSE POWERS OF DEBATE ARE FORMIDABLE, WHO WILL DEFEND YOUR INTERESTS

WITH YOUR BLOOD, WHO TAKES A STAND ON PRINCIPLE ALONE, AND TREATS PERSONAL ATTACKS WITH CONTUMELY. WHOSE KNOWLEDGE OF KAFKA IS BEYOND REPROACH, WHO WILL LEAD YOU FROM THE DARK AGES OF EDUCATION TO THE BROAD UPLANDS OF HOPE, TAKING ON BOARD LOCAL QUESTIONS THE WHILE, WHO WILL SHIRK SERVILE DETAIL IN FAVOUR OF THE BROAD BRUSH, WHO WILL LEAVE YOUR ENVIRONMENT AS HE FOUND IT, WHO WILL ATTACK BOREDOM WHEREVER HE FINDS IT EVEN WITHIN THE VERY FASTNESSES OF OUR OWN ADMINISTRATION.

VOTE FOR MURDO MACRAE, BRING YOUR PROBLEMS TO HIM, AND IF HE IS NOT AT HOME, REMEMBER THAT THIS IS AN INDICATION OF HIS TIRELESS EFFORTS ON YOUR BEHALF.

Murdo on the Problem of Fishing – A Speech

Ladies and gentlemen, fellow members of the proletariat, I wish to say a few words tonight about the problems of the Fishing Industry.

Ever since the dawn of history, men have fished. They have set out in their boats, dhows, piraguas, etc, and sought their food in the wild or temperate oceans. Their families have depended on the flounder, and their kin have espoused the kipper. In Japan men have fished with lanterns and sometimes with the carnivorous cormorant, and in northern climes - interrupted by the Aurora Borealis - the humble kayak has been used.

Later still, as time passed, Columbus set off from Spain after a trifling altercation, towards what he thought was the Indies, with many ships which included the *Santa Maria*. Indomitable man! Fine spirit! Excellent sailor! What did he think of as he progressed further and further into the Pacific without radar or asdic, nay even without compass. What would his thoughts have been as he heard on that bountiful air the first sound of the calypso and smelt the scent of burnt rice.

Later still, after Columbus and Vasca da Gama, whom I did not mention, as time is short, we come to Admiral Horatio Nelson, who fought at Trafalgar, and who it is said was seasick on most of his voyages. You have all heard disapprovingly of his famous last words, 'Kiss me, Hardy.'

As well as this there have been Drake, who played bowls; Sir Walter Raleigh; Amundsen, who discovered the South Pole; Nansen: and many other famous men too numerous to mention. Anecdotes about them abound.

I ask you therefore when you think of such great men, what are your own trifling complaints about boundaries, quotas, tariffs, etc, (stupefaction!) against such a noble panorama of human adventure. (Mutterings of discontent, some in Gaelic.) Nay, listen to me. As the earth turns valiantly in space, as day by day we hear of pulsars and quasars, what can the humble skate do for us. Its status diminishes in comparison with this vast processional and tremendous rotation of the stars. Indeed your drifters, your trawlers, become a mote on the surface of the deep. Do you think Columbus went in search of the squid and was willing to lay down his life for the herring? (Puzzlement!) On the contrary, his lode star was his Imagination; in the rustling of his sails he heard the music of the spheres. What to him the dogfish, the turbot or the crab. Let them stay in their appointed places, he would have said in his Catholic way. (Snarls!)

Men (and women) have laid down their lives for visions, but never for the haddock. The Holy Grail was not in the shape of a kipper nor the North Star in the shape of a swordfish. The sea is a cauldron of invention, gaiety, profusion, more profound than we can imagine. The proletariat were not called to hunt or die for the mackerel, or discuss the dialectics of the plaice. (Howls of rage!) I will be heard, I was trying to raise your consciousness, in this cold hall without electricity or water.

Let me again expatiate on this grand idea. First there was the innocent tree trunk, then the rowing boat, then the sailing ship, then the steamship. What a marvellous procession! Did Nelson face the might of Napoleon thinking of a quota, as he put the telescope to his blind eye? Did Drake, pursuing the Spanish galleon, stop in his tracks as he thought of the tariff? (Disturbance!)

I stand before you here, an honest man, who is trying to assist you and raise your minds to visionary horizons. I prophesy to you: the proletariat will not triumph if they confine their attention to trout. Another net — the net of capitalism, and the relationship of the bourgeois class to its means of production — is closing over you. This matter of fish is merely a red herring to distract you from the theory of surplus value. What do you find in your nets? Not fish but the illusion of profit and counter-revolutionary, adventurist petty bourgeois factionalists. (Baffled snarls!)

You will thank me for this when I am far away, when I am no more. And no less. You will say to yourselves in the twilight of your old age, I wish my consciousness had been raised more. I wish I had listened to his objective analysis instead of being subjective. Why did I not listen to that honest man, you will say, who strove to raise me from my beetle-like condition to the majestic harmonies of the universe. That is roughly what you will meditate on. When you have a home-help you will think of these things. When you are suffering from arthritis and alienation you will remember me perhaps, your friend in hard times, now a dead body in soft times. (A shamed silence!)

I say to you, give up these illusions of quotas, prices, etc. Consider the lilies, how they grow. Stand up and be counted. Remember your wives and children and leave them only fragrant memories uncorrupted by scales and salt. The march of Democracy continues. Turn your faces to the stars, my friends. To the stars. Let you first love your neighbour, and all things will be added to you.

On these aims I rest. (Prolonged cheers!)

TO THE EDITOR OF THE...

Dear Sir,

I see from your correspondence column of last week that H.R.
of Peterhead is objecting to my speech on the Fishing
Industry (so kindly reported by you) and saying that I am
totally ignorant of same.

I think it is scandalous that such an attack should be made by
an outsider, who has no idea at all of the uniqueness of this
community and, if I may say so, its oral tradition and
minority language. What right has he, I ask, to interfere in
our internal affairs. What right has he to expatiate on fishing
affairs in an organ that does not belong to him, and
furthermore against those who have laid down their lives in
two World Wars to defend their own way of life? Let him
look at the mote in his own eye and ask himself, are things so
well conducted in Peterhead that he can afford to attack
others?

I will not, however, be cowed. We have our own mores and
our own culture and we do not wish those with an axe to
grind to interfere.

When I come to the details of his letter I find myself
astonished at his intemperate language. What has Columbus
to do with the Fishing Industry, he asks, and who is Bruno?
I am amazed at his ignorance, quite apart from the fact that

he has singled out Catholics. Is he, perhaps, a member of the Closed Brethren or some such sect that he spews forth his malicious froth.

In the first place, the great names of Columbus and of Bruno (the latter of whom paid the supreme penalty for his beliefs) transcend such matters as he mentions. Would he have stood out against the might of the Pacific or the Inquisition, or would he simply have written a letter to a newspaper? It ill behoves him to attack not only me (for I can disdainfully throw his weak logic back at him) but those who because they are dead cannot defend themselves. If this is meant to be Peterhead fairplay then I comprehensively reject it.

Even in Peterhead he must have heard of the Santa Maria and its famous companions: as also of the burning fire of the Inquisition. Even in Peterhead he must have heard of the well-known statement of Bruno that the universe is infinite. Perhaps it is this that he cannot bear. Does he think that the universe is infinite except in Peterhead and that that town occupies a privileged position? I cannot otherwise account for his poisonous insinuations.

My position in this matter, as on others, is perfectly clear. I believe that at the root of all our problems is the relationship between the historical and the logical in the process of cognition. I come out in favour of the logical method, showing that it made possible the examination of certain categories (including the Fishing Industry) not in the sequence in which they have come to play a decisive role historically, but with an eye on their relationship in contemporary bourgeois society. A correct understanding of existing and extinct forms requires the determination in many instances of decisive forms in the service of logical categories. But it does not follow that I reject the historical method which reproduces phenomena in accordance with their actual historical sequence. "The anatomy of man is a key to the anatomy of the ape."

It is of course from such a standpoint that my analysis of the Fishing Industry can best be understood. Simplistic solutions cannot stand the test of time any more than the hollowed-out tree-trunk can carry passengers in the 20th century. Homer too is very different from Picasso.

I hope, sir, my correspondent from Peterhead will clearly understand my position and realise that I have no personal animus towards him but towards his outdated ideology. (Has he, for instance, read the special supplement to the Neue Rheinishe Zeitung, No. 143, issued in 1848 Nov. 15 for his information.) His mistake lies in adopting a subjective stance instead of an objective one, and in not drawing the correct conclusions from the phenomena. In this he is to be found with the discredited Thierry, Proudhon, etc, petty-bourgeois all of them and blatant adventurists. Let him remember these famous words, "The direst straits are better than public begging" and also: "The National Assembly has its seat in the people and not in the confines of this or that heap of stones."

Sir, we are all responsible to the people, and let H.R. of Peterhead keep that in mind.

> *I am, Sir.*
> *Yours, etc,*
> *Murdo Macrae.*

MURDO & THE SPACESHIP

When I arrived at Murdo's house I found him working on a big machine while another man was sitting on a chair with a melodeon. Murdo's daughter, Mary, was asking him how the spaceship was coming...

Murdo said, 'I need paraffin. Morag doesn't have any in the shop. She's got everything else, spades, rinso, mince, bread, margarine, guided missiles, but no paraffin.' His thick glasses glittered contemptuously.

'Well, I'm sure it won't be long till you get your paraffin,' said Mary. 'Do you need anything else?'

'I need four inch nails,' said her father, 'but Kenneth here got them for me in New York. He was playing at a Gaelic festival there, weren't you, Kenneth?'

'Indeed I was,' said Kenneth, who was bald and had a very thin neck.

'Kenneth here is a sex symbol,' said Murdo. 'He was playing at this festival and he went into a shop in 42nd Street. The man who owned it was from Skye. It took him three years to reach America on MacBrayne's and then he was attacked by some Red Indians from Harris. Isn't that right, Kenneth?'

'That's right,' said Kenneth.

'And what are you going to do with the spaceship, father?' said Mary.

'It's not a spaceship. It's a rocket,' said Murdo. 'I thought at first of directing it against Moscow but then I thought Moscow hasn't done anything to me so I'll attack MacBraynes with it instead.'

'It's high time you launched the rocket, father,' said Mary. 'I can't reach the wardrobe because of it.'

'The wardrobe,' said Murdo.

'Yes, where I keep the clothes.'

'Oh, the wardrobe. I can't understand how you can think of trivialities like that in this technological age,' said Murdo. 'Surely you know that I have spent seven years on this project. Seven years when I could have been doing something else.'

'Like what?' said Mary.

'Well, building an anti-ballistic shield,' said Murdo.

'When do you intend to launch the rocket?' said Mary.

At that point a little woman dressed in black and carrying a Bible bound with elastic came in.

'Oh, here's Anna,' said Murdo. 'Were you in church, Anna?'

'Yes, indeed,' said Anna. 'The text was from Exodus. A good minister. Strong voice. Fine hairstyle.'

'What did you say?' said Murdo.

'Oh, I'm in a rage,' Anna said, 'Jessie was wearing the same kind of hat as me.'

After a while, Murdo said in a serious voice, 'Anna.'

'Yes,' said Anna.

'Would you like to go to the moon, Anna?'

'To the moon?' said Anna, in a surprised voice.

'Surely, father, you're not sending Anna to the moon,' said Mary. 'You promised me I could go to the moon. I bought a new frock for it.'

'You keep quiet, Mary,' said Murdo angrily.

He turned to Anna. 'The thing is, Anna, do you think

you'd be able to handle the media? The media is very important.'

'Media? What's that?' said Anna.

'The newspapers, the BBC, the television,' said Murdo.

'Oh, I can speak to them right enough,' said Anna. 'What do I have to say?'

'Father,' said Mary.

'You keep quiet,' said Murdo. 'I want a religious woman to land on the moon. A woman who can sing a psalm. Can you do that, Anna?'

'Oh, I can sing a psalm right enough,' said Anna. 'But you want me to do it on the moon?'

'Think of it, Anna,' said Murdo. 'You'll be standing on the moon, in your black mini-skirt with your fish-net stockings. Real fish-net. Of course, we'll take the corks out of it first. You will be a sex symbol for the whole world.'

'I would like that,' said Anna.

'And now for the big day,' said Murdo, taking out his diary. 'It can't be Thursday. That's early closing day. Or Sunday. You can't go to the moon on a Sunday, Anna.'

'No, I couldn't do that,' said Anna.

'Tuesday would be all right,' said Murdo. 'Are you free on Tuesday?'

'Tuesday,' said Anna. 'Oh, I don't know about Tuesday. That's my Hate the Catholics night.'

'Well, what about Wednesday then?' said Murdo. 'You don't go to the bingo on a Wednesday, do you?'

'No, I don't go to the bingo,' said Anna. 'Wednesday would be all right.'

'I'll put that in my diary then,' said Murdo. 'You're not frightened are you.'

'Not at all,' said Anna.

'And you're not afraid of communicating with the media? You must be sharp and quick, Anna. What will you say to them when they ask you why you joined the mission to the moon?'

'I'll say, this is a big step for mankind but especially for Gravir.'

'Oh, there is one other thing,' said Murdo. 'Is there anything suspicious or immoral in your background, Anna? You can expect a lot of probing. The media is ruthless.'

'Immoral?' said Anna.

'Yes, like incest, murder, theft, speaking to Catholics. Anything like that?'

'No, no,' said Anna, 'nothing at all like that.'

'That's good, Anna. And now we'll sing Amazing Grace. What about Amazing Grace, Kenneth? Give us Amazing Grace.'

Kenneth sang Amazing Grace, but not well. 'It's all right, said Murdo. 'Kenneth here is more used to Country and Western. What's wrong, Anna?'

'I've just remembered. I can't go on Wednesday.'

'Why not?' said Murdo.

'It's the day I collect my pension,' said Anna.

Murdo gnashed his teeth with frustration and chased her out.

'That means Mary here will have to go after all,' he said.

Murdo & his Candidate

The results of the election were:

Mr R. Green	*500*
Mr Chevenix Trench	*150*
Mr Murdo Macrae	*2*

Murdo immediately demanded a recount but the result was upheld.

He wrote a letter to the local paper in which he said:

To these two supporters of mine in the recent election (Ward 3) I wish to say Courage. As yet our ideas have not won wide credence, but was this not the same with many movements in the past? And these later proved of course to be of major significance. One thinks of the Children's Crusade, etc.

Popularity is easily won in these materialistic times, when men will promise the earth, but when one is concerned with a new heaven and a new earth what price votes and ballot boxes then? Do not, I say, be downcast, for I am not downcast. I shall return to the fray, refreshed and patriotic as usual.

The very fact that I only got two votes suggests to me not that my ideas are without substance but that they are ahead of their time. Popularity, as I have said, is easily won and the world will soon know the emptiness of Mr R. Green's ideas, such as they are, when they are tested in the furnace of local politics and , if I may say so, the fires of reality.

I salute you therefore, my two supporters, for your percipience and your honesty. Only you were able to pierce through the prevailing fog of lies and distortion to the inner meaning of my proposals. Only you are the true metaphysicians of democracy. I wish I knew who you were. Sometimes I think of you as idealistic, ardent, blazing with fervour. I think of you also as ones who eschew popularity in favour of Truth, hermits contemptuous of the world of electricity and fake progress around you.

Withal, I think of you as young, independent-minded, not easily convinced. Not for you the rigid forms of the old politics, no, you wish to say to these malignant masks, Avaunt. Get thee behind me.

I say to you in Macarthur's immortal words spoken, I think, to the Filipinos or some such Pacific tribe, "I shall return." And return I shall to cleanse these Augean stables and begin again, as we make our way towards the stars.

Thank you again, my dear friends, for your faith in me.

> I am,
> Yours, etc,
> Murdo Macrae.

PS. To Mr R. Green I say, with the inner rage and contempt of the temporary loser,

WE ARE WATCHING YOU: WE WILL NOT REST TILL YOUR CONTEMPTIBLE IDEAS ARE CONSIGNED TO THE DUST-BIN OF HISTORY, WHERE THEY UNDOUBTEDLY BELONG.

Murdo & the Mod

At the time of the Mod, Murdo tended to get into long arguments about Mod medallists. He would say, 'In my opinion Moira Mcinally was the best medallist there ever was. Her timbre was excellent.' Most people wouldn't know what timbre was, and Murdo would repeat the word. On the other hand, he would say that though her timbre was excellent her deportment wasn't as good as that of Norma McEwan who became a bus conductress on the Govan route.

Such arguments would go on into the early hours of the morning, and as many as eighty Mod medallists might be mentioned with special reference to their expression when they sang their songs, as well as their marks in Gaelic and music. Murdo would sometimes say, '97 out of 100 is not enough for a medallist since I myself used to get more than that in Geometry.'

'However,' he would add, 'Mairi MacGillivary got 99 out of 100 for her timbre, though she only got 7 out of 100 for her Gaelic since in actual fact she was a learner and was born in Japan.'

'Her expression,' he would add, 'was enigmatic.'

At one Mod he offered protection for adjudicators. This was a service which consisted of whisking them off to an armoured taxi immediately they had given their adjudication. For he said, 'Haven't you realised the number of threats those adjudicators get? Not so often from the contestants themselves but from their close relatives, especially their mothers who have carefully trained these contestants for many years in expression, timbre, and the best method of wearing the kilt. No one has any idea of what is involved in producing a gold medallist. His Gaelic must be perfection itself as far as expression is concerned and must be taken from the best islands. Furthermore, he must stand in a particular way with his hand on his sporran, and his expression must be fundamentally alert, though not impudent, though for the dreamier songs he may close his eyes. Now a mother who has brought up such a contestant cannot but be angry when an adjudicator, who doesn't even come from her island, presumes to make her son fifth equal in a contest which moreover only contains fifth equals. There have been death threats in the past. Some adjudicators have disguised themselves as members of the Free Church and carry Bibles and wear black hats and black ties, but this isn't enough as everyone knows that the Free Church doesn't like Mods, since they are not mentioned in the Bible. The *Comunn Gaidhealach* have even produced very thin adjudicators who, as it were, melt into the landscape when their adjudication is over, but even this has not prevented them from being assaulted. These mothers will stand in freezing rain outside adjudicators' houses and shout insults at them and sometimes the more ambitious of them have fired mortar shells into the living-room.'

Thus Murdo's "Adjudicators Rescue Service", knows as ARS for short, was in great demand, and for an extra pound the adjudicator could make faces at frenzied mothers through the bullet-proof glass.

Another service that Murdo would provide was skin-coloured hearing aids which in practical terms were in fact invisible. These were for turning off after the seventh hearing of the same song, such as "Bheir Mi Ho." If the hearing aids were visible it would look discourteous to turn them off. So Murdo would advertise for people who would make skin-coloured invisible hearing aids, and sometimes he would even apply for a grant for such people who had to be highly skilled and whose pay was high as they only worked during Mod times.

Another service he provided was special tartans for people from Russia and Japan and other distant countries. His tartan for the Oblomov clan was well thought of. It was a direct and daring perestroika white with a single dove carrying a Mod brochure in its mouth. Sometimes too it might carry a placard "Welcome to Mod 1992 in Dazzling and Riveting Kilmarnock, home of Gaelic and Engineering Sponsorship." Indeed his sponsorship from Albania was the high point of his life, and he kept for a long time a transcript of the short interview he had with its president, who at that time was being besieged by 300,000 rebellious people demanding more soap and toilet paper.

Murdo indeed became very animated at the time of the Mod, as if he were emerging out of a long hibernation like the church at Easter. He ran a service well in advance of the Mod for booking Choirs into Bed and Breakfast locations, and he further advertised a service for making rooms soundproof so that pipers could practise their pibrochs, one of which was in fact dedicated to him. It was called *Murdo's Farewell to Harry Lauder*. He invented a device by which a piper could smoke while playing the pipes at the same time. He advertised this by the slogan "Put that in your pipes and smoke it."

But I could go on for ever describing Murdo's energy and innovative brilliance at the time of the Mod. It was as if he grew alive again, as if he vibrated with elan.

He was here, there and everywhere, organising dances, selling tickets, raffling salt herring, giving endless votes of thanks, singing songs, defending the Mod in midnight debates, pinpointing the virtues of Mod gold medallists of earlier years and interviewing them in a special geriatric studio which was fitted with bedpans, dressing up as a starving Campbell who needed sponsorship, writing short stories and sending them in under assumed names such as Iain MacRae Hemingway or Hector Maupassant. It was a week of glorious abandon for him, so much so that the rest of the year was an anticlimax, and he could hardly wait until the Mod was to be staged in Gatwick or Henley.

Murdo's closely reasoned paper on why the Mod should be held in Paris was probably his masterpiece. He said first of all that many of the older slightly deafer people might think it was Harris, and before they knew where they were they would be strolling down the Champs Elysees rather than Tarbert. Also there were a number of Gaels in Paris who had been detained there after the last football international as well as some ancient followers of Bonnie Prince Charlie. Furthermore, it was probably from here that the original Celts had come before they had changed from "P" to "Q". Also the word "église" was very like the Gaelic word "eaglais" and there was a small French religious sect called L'Eglise Libre to which Pascal had belonged.

So it was that Murdo was busy as a bee when Mod time came, especially with his compilation of Mod medallists into leagues, headed by Morag MacCrimmon (aged 102), and by his selection of raffle prizes headed by his special editions of the Bible with a foreword by Nicholas Fairbairn, and a page three of aged schoolteachers from the Stornoway Gazette.

'I envisage,' he told the press recently, 'that our next Mod will be in East Germany. As a goodwill gesture I have decided that there will be no communists on the committee. I hope to see you all there.'

I should like, but for pressure of time, to detail Murdo's other astonishing achievements, e.g. the year he won the Mod Medal himself by an amazing margin of 90 points, and also his epic poem which won him the Bardic Crown and which was called "The Church and the Sound of the Sea." However, I have said enough to demonstrate that Murdo was by far the most interesting President, Secretary, and Treasurer seen at the same time which the Mod is ever likely to have, and his creation of twenty fourth-equals out of a total entry of twenty-one was the most dazzling arithmetical feat ever seen and also the fairest.

His interview in Gaelic with President Mitterand was a sparkling performance when he countered the President's *"Tha e fluich"* with *"C'est la guerre."*

MURDO'S XMAS LETTER

Dear Friends,

Another Christmas has come again, and I am sending you a report of my activities during the year. It doesn't seem so long ago since last Christmas was here, but as we all know it is twelve months ago — no more and no less.

My main project in the early part of the year was to encourage Scottish writing, by running a competition for short stories. I asked for a sum of ten pounds to be enclosed with each story: this was to cover administrative costs, coffee, stamps, and whisky, etc. The prizes which I presented in March were ten pounds for the best story, one pound for the next story and 10p for third best. I hope to do something similar for Scottish Writing next year. I shall advise entrants that a maximum of 200 words is entirely reasonable, as it seems to me that one of the faults of Scottish Writing is that it is too long, and with shorter short stories I shall be able to apply better my critical techniques. Far more emphasis should be placed on the single word, which is the hallmark of the truly great writer. What I look for first is good typing, then originality.

Another project in which I was involved gave me great satisfaction. I have noticed in the past that the standards of In Memoriams in the local paper is very low, and it seems to me that with a little practice they could be improved. I therefore started a workshop for that purpose. I told my class that epitaphs have concentrated mainly on names and dates,

*without referring in depth to the individual nature of the
dead person. I told them that the best writing of the
twentieth century is above all truthful. Thus if the dead
person was highly sexed, perverted, or a habitual thief, this
should be stated. As a result of our final workshop (the cost
for the whole course was £50 to each member) I shall put
together a small anthology of the best In Memoriams.*

Here are two examples:

"May James Campbell's randy bones rest in peace."

and

*"May John MacDonald be able to find his way to his own
grave."*

The classic, I think, was

"Let her RIP."

*I may say that the sales of the local newspaper have soared
since these epitaphs were inserted and I had a congratulatory
message from the editor.*

*Old clothes is another area of my research, the idea for which
I got from the local Oxfam. I have started a campaign by
which I hope to convince people that old clothes are better
than new ones. The logic of my argument goes like this.
Community, I say, is the basis of our life here in the island,
and what would be more communal than to wear clothes
which in the past have been worn by someone else. In this
way we inherit history, sweat, stains and genealogy. Old
clothes are like a time machine: they give an insight into the
past that cannot be gained in any other way. Look, I say, at
these rags which better men and women than you have worn.
They did not know where their next meal was coming from.
Indeed they did not know where their last meal had come
from. Do you not wish to have thoughts like them, pure
healthy thoughts, and not impure unhealthy thoughts such as
people who wear new clothes have?*

Such people, I say, existed on bread and sour milk. Many of my hearers, and I don't blame them for this, have been so moved by my rhetoric that they have stripped off their new clothes on the spot and have taken old clothes of a similar size. This, I say, is what Christianity was really about. Did Christ shop at Harrods? Such a statement has only to be made for the absurdity of it to be revealed. Nor in fact has anyone found an answer to my logic and I do not think anyone will.

So you see, my friends, that I have not been idle.

I have also decided during the course of this year to change the subject of my novel. It was originally to be about a bank clerk, but I have noticed on television a resurgence of the detective story. Thus I have created a private eye called Sam Spaid who walks, as I write, the mean streets of Portree. He wears a bowler hat, and when he is in his office listens to tapes of Free Church sermons. He doesn't drink or smoke and his only vice is sniffing. In his first case he opened his door to find a stunning Free Church woman there. He immediately knew that she spelt trouble. The elastic which she kept round her Bible had been stolen. This investigation, which of course ended in success, took Sam Spaid to a cache of black elastic in Inverness. Sam Spaid's fee, which never varies, is £20 per day plus expenses! He will never be rich but he will be an interesting moral phenomenon. His next case will involve the serial murders of Free Church ministers by a crazed sniper who was made to spend his early years in the Sunday School.

I hope you are not bored at hearing about my projects at great length but at this season of the year such ramblings may be forgiven, as Christmas carols are.

My final project has to do with a taxi service that I run for drunks at the New Year. For this purpose I have a number of advertisements run off, which read, "Drink as much as you like. Murdo will run you home." In small print it reads, "Ditches, lavatories, cemeteries, scoured for those who have INDULGED too much." The taxi is of course my own car and I am happy for it to be used for such a Christian purpose. In the course of this work I have become very humble, as I have been beaten up and vomited on many times. Hence I have developed a servile stance which has served me well. I call my customers "Sir" or "My Lord" and am especially friendly to large people, and to those whose jackets are flecked with a mixture of lager and sickness. It seems to me reasonable that I should charge extra for taking people to their doors or to their lavatories or even to their bedrooms. I wear protective clothing and sometimes a gas-mask. I charge also for burns from cigarettes on the seat of my car. I consider what I am doing to be a Christian duty which money in itself cannot pay. I could tell you of some little contretemps I have had, as for example a drug-crazed addict from Shawbost who attacked me with a graip, but I shall refrain. Nor will I mention that time I took one of my customers to the wrong bedroom. This arose from the fact that there are many Norman MacLeods on the island.

As you can see therefore I have had a busy and eventful year. Blessings on you wherever you are and may we exchange literature such as this often in the future.

Yours as ever

Murdo

MURDO AND BURNS

Murdo was once asked to make the Immortal Speech to Robert Burns, as the man who was supposed to give it fell ill because of the weight of the task assigned to him.

'Ladies and gentlemen, much has already been written and said about Burns. Burns and the Church, Burns and Freedom, Burns and the '45, Burns and Friendship, Burns and Dogs. All these have been speculated on by greater orators than I. Tonight I wish to speak on the topic of Burns and Mice.

Let us think for a moment about mice. They are tiny animals who penetrate our houses and raid our larders. They breed very quickly, as we are told. Cats seize them and kill them. But it is not often that we see the world from the point of view of the mouse. To mice we human beings must appear giants, greedy, vast and implacable. Whenever we see a mouse we wish to kill it. Why therefore should the mouse have any respect for us? Indeed, why should it not despise us, for in its deepest self it is a pacifist. And yet "an icker in a thrave" is all that it wants from us. Now in the time of Burns there were no traps; it has fallen to us sophisticated beings to have created such things. All that Burns had was a ploughshare.

Let us therefore picture the mouse. A mouse whom we cannot know individually — for mice do not have names as we have — runs trembling from the ploughshare that the great poet is using, for we know that he was a farmer. It is not to our present purpose to ask whether he was a good or bad farmer: that is a matter for literary critics.

The mouse, we are told, is running away "wi' bickerin brattle." A fine phrase in itself. Here it is, naked and grey, among the corn, and there is the great poet, who had by this time written many great poems. It is not a minor poet that we have here but a major poet at the height of his powers or as we might say "pooers". Most great poets would not see in this tiny creature matter for speculation. A mouse? Who would address a mouse? Burns would. And that is why he is our National Poet. At this moment he would teach us a lesson. A mouse and a great poet would be equal, for, as he himself wrote. "A Man's a Man for a' that." This is not a poet who despised mice, this is one who studied them.

Nor did he assail this mouse for stealing his corn, though he might well have done so. Thief, he might have shouted, as we ourselves might have under similar circumstances, with this proviso, however, that we are not Burns, a lad that was born in Kyle and who wrote among other things, "My Love is Like a Red Red Rose." One who himself knew destitution, poverty — and corn.

The mouse, as we may imagine, did not wait for Burns to deliver his poem. It ran away, for that is the nature of the mouse. It does not wait to find out what the great poet will do with the ploughshare. Burns meanwhile stands there astonished. The divine afflatus has descended upon him, for his Muse does not despise a mouse.

Is there here not a lesson for us all?

What indeed may "a bickerin brattle" not signify. May it not call us to be human beings? And what indeed is "an icker in a thrave." All of us can afford one. We are not so poor that we cannot afford "an icker." We may of course be so armoured in the luxuries of the world that we feel we cannot do so, but if we think for a moment we find we can.

Now the next thing to be said is that by the time Burns is composing his poem the mouse has disappeared. It will not wait for the great poet. On the contrary it will escape, for has it not known of the hardness of the world? Of course it has: and Burns too knows that, for he has seen and known many mice.

Burns therefore is present and the mouse is not. That is a paradox in itself and all great poetry is full of paradoxes. And we cannot imagine the mouse, an icker in its paws, caught red-handed as it were, awaiting for Burns to address it, however attractive that picture might be. Did Burns at that moment remember his dear Jean — all his dear loves, even Clarinda? Did he recall his first fumbling attempts at verse, as he stared at the place where the mouse had been, and now was no more? We don't know: we cannot know — but I think he did. I think as the helpless mouse ran away that he thought of all these things, and of his efforts to succeed in farming, and of his future career in Customs and Excise, and perhaps even of the French Revolution which raged fiercely at that time.

I will not chase thee with my murderin' pattle, Burns said to the mouse. I may chase other beings but not you. My pattle will be kept for dealing with others as the occasion may arise but not you, you helpless being. And the mouse, hiding somewhere, must have been aware of all this. He must have been in his mouselike mind aware that a great decision had been made by Burns. The great poet would not, as in a manic rage, rush into the corn and wave his pattle furiously. We do not know if the mouse knew what a pattle was: perhaps not. Suffice it to say that it was safe at least from the pattle of Burns.

Then we see that Burns was drawn to the wee bit hoosie now in ruin. It is not simply the mouse that he has to be concerned with, but its tiny tenement. And Burns knew of this, for he himself had been forced to change houses as his land failed. His house was in ruin and the wind, snell and keen blew through it, though of course it had no windows. Burns indeed mourned — for man is made to mourn — but what else could he have done? Was he to know that this tiny tenement was in the path of his ploughshare? No indeed: and therefore he need not blame himself.

But the point of this great poem is that he did! This great poet did! With his ploughshare he had laid that tiny tenement low. And he was sorry for it. He regretted it. And he mourned too for the mouse. And he stood there shivering, for in those days they did not have the thermal clothing that we now have — nor indeed would he have deigned to wear it, for he was a proud passionate man whom wet weather would not frighten, and that is of course why he died at such an early age, of rheumatic fever, as we are told — and he stood there shivering like the mouse. Both the mouse and the great poet shivering. What a picture fit for the heart we have here. And beside them is the cruel coulter. And the mouse and the man have to thole the cranreuch. What poetry is in these words, for "cranreuch", as we know, is the Scots word for frost.

Ladies and gentlemen, I find myself moved at this moment. Here we have a great poet who has written poems like "The Banks of Ayr", "For the Sake of Somebody" and "Charlie is My Darling", and many more such gems, face to face with the vanished mouse, and one of the greatest moments of his life is here. Did he shrink away from it? No, he did not. On the contrary he showed, this passionate man, feelings that the rest of the world would not show towards a mouse. He was not ashamed to weep in that cranreuch cauld. With his murderin' pattle he stood there, not ashamed to weep, this great poet who had been let down by this brother Gilbert, who knew, as scholars have reminded us, French, and who was au fait, as scholars have also reminded us, with the contemporary work of Pope and others of that ilk. Ladies and gentlemen, I cannot – or canna – but weep as I see this great poet shivering in that field, as important as Bannockburn. A mouse and a great poet. Not indeed two warriors facing each other with wrath and anger, but a great poet and a mouse, an odd confrontation withal. '

Murdo looked around him. That majestic audience, touched to the quick, was weeping. He paused and then said in ringing tones,

'Please be upstanding. Robert Burns.' And then again in hushed reverent tones, 'Robert Burns.'

Then he sat down to the plaudits of the assembled multitudes who had been stunned and moved by his eloquence, his understanding, his sensitivity, his extraordinary insight into the psychology of the mouse. When afterwards they all came to clap him on the shoulder, and say 'Weill dune', over and over again, he muttered humbly, 'Burns – the mouse.' And wiped, as it were, a tear from his eye. But at the same time he accepted all the whiskies he was offered, for this was after all a poetic occasion.

Murdo's Application for a Bursary

Dear Sir,

I wish to apply for a bursary from you in order that I may complete my book **Down the Mean Streets of Portree.** *This is a detective story in which the private eye is a member of the Free Church. His name is Sam Spaid, and he is a convinced Presbyterian. I do not see why the Catholics should have Father Brown and we Protestants nobody. I have written a few pages, which I enclose. These are only a first draft and I hope to complicate the cases further by introducing the idea of Predestination and the Elect, etc. This first case is called "The Mess of Pottage."*

I notice from your letter that you require a referee to substantiate my application. As you will understand, I live here in a very isolated situation, and referees who are competent to judge my work are thin on the ground. I thought at first of the headmaster and the minister, but the headmaster for various complicated reasons does not speak to me, and the minister would not approve of my novel. I have, however, a neighbour who is a simple crofter and whose name is Malcolm Campbell. He is an honest man, owner of a few acres of land, and he is quite willing to be my referee. Please excuse his writing as he is not one of these people who will put his signature to anything. He has a view of life which is unsophisticated and true. Thus though he does not understand the finer minutiae of my work, he knows me well enough to appreciate that I would not put in false claims. He is a regular reader of the Bible and Robert Burns and some selected parts of Spurgeon, and what better literary background could one have? Also he wishes me to get the grant as I owe him a trifling sum for certain repairs he made to my draughty house some time ago. I have tidied up this application a little as he left school at 15 years of age. It is good, as you will appreciate, to have such staunch friends in adversity.

I see also that you require a note of income. Last year I made £200 altogether. Most of this was the income from a Short Story Competition which I ran, in order to encourage Scottish Writing. The rest was in the form of a workshop on "In Memoriams" which was not as lucrative as I expected.

I have other projects as well. One of my stories requires that Sam Spaid go to Peru in order to capture a criminal who has been trying to undercut the Bible market. I hope to apply for a Travel Grant for that, as of course I would need to study the laws, the social mores, etc, for authentic detail. There is a scene where Sam Spaid confronts a Peruvian god which will require considerable research. I am at the moment trying to find out how much bed and breakfast costs in Lima. Another project of mine involves a visit by Sam Spaid to Israel. This has to do with a secret weapon a crazed member of the Free Church congregation is importing in stages from a fanatical Jewish sect. I will, however, keep in touch with you about this.

There is one other project I am working on as well. In past years some of the islanders when working with The Hudson Bay Company, married and brought home Cree women. Now, the psychology of these women when confronted by our island ways has not been sufficiently investigated. Was the Cree woman frightened, puzzled, enthralled? Did her thoughts return to tepees, pipes of peace, tomahawks, memories of buffalo, etc? There is much research to be done on this;

indeed none at all has been done.

It is not enough to say that perhaps only two such women appeared on the island. Two is quite enough for my financial purposes, and if numbers were to be the final arbiter what would we say of the victory of the heavily outnumbered Athenians at Marathon. And furthermore on such a premise our ideas of democracy would be in dire jeopardy, as a moment's thought is enough to show. How indeed are the thoughts, griefs, joys, etc, of one Cree woman any less important than our own? She too had her ambitions, melancholy, and elations. She too had her fears and her hopes. As she saw the sun rise in the morning over the Muirneag, memories of her home on the plain must have returned to her, of her aged chieftain father, various mothers, and so on. And she must also have thought of the young brave from whom her religious husband tore her, to take her to a strange and barbarous island where a minority language was spoken. As you can see, therefore, I have many projects on hand.

I also note that you require a track record of publication. The reason why I have published nothing is very clear. First of all, I am a perfectionist and secondly I am not greatly impressed by the magazines I see on bookstalls. Their stories and poems seem to me to lack a central plan such as I myself have, though I have not put it on paper yet. This vision glimmers before me day and night, and I try in vain to grasp it. It seems to me that these inferior writers have grasped their ideas and put them on paper too soon. Decades, generations, centuries, are not enough for me to grasp this vision. And indeed only my need for financial security — for bread, payment of council tax, payment of new carpet — forces me to frame it in a narrow compass now. It is for visions such as these that you should be paying, intangible, magnificent visions which indeed may come to nothing, but which on the other hand may result in unexpected masterpieces. I often feel that you are lacking in faith, if I may venture a criticism, and that you snatch at the inferior manuscript when you should be supporting the visionary and as yet unwritten text.

However, that is by the bye, and I hope I have not offended you in any way. Beggars such as I cannot be choosers, and great, though as yet unidentified success, leaves a salt taste on the tongue. A pair of trousers, a slice of bread, may be lost by true and sincere criticism. Furthermore, there are many talents born to blush unseen and waste their sweetness on the desert air. It might be that had your organisation existed in the eighteenth century, Robert Burns might have applied for a bursary and lived to a hale old age, where he would have written companions to such deathless poems as "To a Mouse". And John Keats might have done the same as well. And Shelley, if he had not been drowned.

If you will bear with me for a moment I will share with you my vision of what an Arts Council should be. Instead of asking for samples and incomes, it should be a source of largesse. It should be the DHSS of the aspiring writer till such time as he can get into print. For he may — and this is where the act of faith comes in — write a masterpiece. Could an early Arts Council have foreseen Paradise Lost or The Divine Comedy? Did even Homer see the Iliad in advance? The logic is irrefutable. The Arts Council should give a bursary to all applicants in case a potential Catullus is neglected.

I return to democracy again. Even one Lucretius or Sir Thomas Wyatt would be a justification of such a policy. Therefore, I appeal to you in the name of such a vision, open your purses: give, give, give, even to those who cannot provide samples, but who have exciting visions of the future. For it may be that by asking for samples you are toadying to the opportunist and the materialist. Is it not in fact in his interests to provide such samples? Are there not inducements for him to do so? But what of the awkward unspeaking one, *who is possessed by a vision that he cannot put on paper. What of him? Is he to be ignored in favour of the smooth con-man? Those great inarticulate ones of whom the Statue of Liberty speaks, are they not to be brought to your arms? — I think they are.*

I say, think of these things, and I hope also that this letter is not too long, and that what I have said may be taken on board. I know that inflation eats into your budget and I know also that the going rate for a bursary at the moment is £5,000.

Yours in anticipation,
Murdo Macrae

THE MESS OF POTTAGE

Sam Spaid was reading the second chapter of Deuteronomy when there was a timid knock at the door.

'Come in', he shouted, closing his Bible reluctantly.

A small woman, wearing a black hat, black coat, and shoes from Macdonald and Sons, Portree, entered. She stood with her hands folded, her gaze fixed on the floor, away from the great detective. He recognised her at once: she was Annie Macleod who sat three rows behind him in the church every Sunday.

'You look ill,' he said, 'would you like a cup of water? I don't keep coffee.'

'No thank you,' she said.

'Is there anything wrong?' he said, drawing out for her the chair he kept for clients, for he knew at once that she was a client.

How can she afford me, he thought, but put the thought away from him at once.

Suddenly she said, 'It's my husband Donnie. He's run away.'

Donnie, he thought, that sinful atheist. Aloud, he said, 'Run away?'

'I know he has. He left a note saying, "I've had enough".'

Sam took the note, but not before he had equipped himself with a pair of black woollen gloves, also from Macdonald and Sons, Portree.

'You are sure this is his handwriting?'

'Yes I am sure. You will notice his spelling of "enuff".'

'I see,' said Sam. 'I can tell little from this note except that it is from the edge of a newspaper, and that it is clearly the work of a disturbed man. What is this?' and he lent forward, scenting a clue. 'A spot of red.'

'It might be blood,'said Annie timidly. 'He might have cut himself shaving.'

'Not while he wrote the note,' said Sam contemptuously. 'No, this spot is something more sinister than that. However, you may continue.'

His eyes took in the woman's worn coat. No, there would not be much money to be made from this case.

'After all I have done for him.' said Annie, taking out a small white handkerchief and dabbing her eyes. 'It was I who introduced him to the blessing of the Gospel. I used to read a chapter of the Bible to him every night. I talked to him about his sinful life. Whenever he was backsliding I prayed for his soul.'

'And?' said Sam keenly.

'Recently. I noticed a change in him. When I read to him he would stare into space or click his teeth. Sometimes he would mutter to himself. He spent a lot of time in his room. I think he had a woman in there.'

'What makes you think that?'

'Perfume, powder, things like that.'

'Who could this woman be? Did he go out much?'

'He didn't go out at all. I also found a pile of magazines under his bed. Unspeakable. Naked men and women...' She paused for a moment.

'You did not bring them with you?' said Sam.

'No, I did not think you...'

'They would have been evidence,' said Sam curtly. Why did he have to tell these people everything? Why, since the Clearances, could they not think for themselves? He felt his toothache beginning again. He wanted to hit this woman. Why don't you fight? he wanted to shout at her.

'Did you bring a photograph?' he asked.

'No, I thought you knew...'

'I do, I do, but a photograph would have been useful. People change, you know.'

'But you only saw him last week.'

'Did I? Maybe I did. But I wasn't observing. Observation is everything.' Again he felt a twinge of hatred for this woman who was sitting so docilely in front of him.

'How long have you been married?' he asked irrelevantly.

'Thirty years. I met him when I was coming out of the Claymore Hotel. He was in fact drunk and shouting at the people who were passing. From that moment I decided to save him. I was thirty-five, and all my suitors had left me because I was too religious.'

'So you are in fact older than him.'

'By ten years. But that was not a barrier at first,' and she smiled.

Enough of this, you contemptible woman, Sam thought bitterly. He himself had been married once, but his wife had left him when he had become a detective. Her figure with its black costume, and shoes from Macdonald and Sons, Portree, haunted him still. He pushed the thought away from him.

'I charge £20 a day plus expenses,' he said sharply.

'£20 a day. But how could I ... Donnie was on the dole and I have my pension.'

'Do you want him back or don't you?' said Sam in a frenzy of rage, though his voice was outwardly calm. He felt a twinge of his arthritis starting. Out of the window he could see people making their way to the Co-op next door as if nothing was happening. This is my domain, he meditated, this is the mean street down which I must go. This is where I must come to, after my childhood. He pondered the delights of predestination.

'I will find the money somehow,' said Annie pathetically.

'Good,' said Sam. 'Now you may go.' As she left he had the most intense desire to throw at her the paperweight that was lying on the desk. Highlanders! Would they never learn to give correct efficient evidence? Would they always accept their fate? Why would they not fight for their identity? For their language?

He adjusted his bowler hat and suit from Macdonald and Sons, as he stared into the sinful mirror in front of him. He threw a last look at the photograph of the Rev. John Macdonald which sat on the wall, and made his way down to the pier, where the ferry was waiting.

'Any news?' said Norman MacMillan, who had a pile of tickets in his hand.

'Only the good news of the Gospel,' said Sam curtly. 'I would like to ask you, when did you see Donnie Macleod last?'

'Donnie Macleod,' said Norman a few times.

(You slow thinking spud, thought Sam savagely, are you some kind of inanimate cabbage? He wanted to kick Norman MacMillan in the shin.)

The wheel of Norman's mind ground to a halt. 'Yes,' he said. 'Funnily enough I saw him yesterday. He was on the ferry.'

'Was he carrying a case?' asked Sam.

There was another long silence in which Sam visualised a torture machine of the most marvellous complexity.

'He was, and I thought it funny at the time.'

(Why did you think it funny at the time? He was on a ferry, wasn't he?)

'Did he look worried?'

'Worried? Worried? Worried? No, he didn't look worried. He said a strange thing to me though. A very strange thing. You must know that I do not know Donnie well. He hasn't left the house for years. His father, as you remember, was that Angus Macleod who went suddenly mad and jumped over the side of the ferry...'

(These oral stories, thought Sam savagely. This tradition they pride themselves on — how can a detective exist in such an environment. His eye rested on a bollard and he wished he could heave it out of the stone and hammer Norman's bald head with it.)

'...not of course that many people speak about it now. But anyway he was standing just about where you are, or perhaps a little to the left, and he said, "A change is good for a man", just as I was taking his ticket and he was making his way to the ferry. And he looked odd.'

'Odd. What do you mean by odd?'

'What do I mean by odd? I mean odd. His eyes were flashing. That's the only way I can describe it. Flashing.'

(You retarded idiot, thought Sam. That's the only way you can describe it. Of course it is. You were never well-known for your discriminate style.)

'And then,' Norman said, leaning forward and speaking in a whisper, 'his very words were, "A change is good for a man."' Norman withdrew his head so quickly that he nearly butted Sam in the face, while at the same time his left eye winked rapidly at the great detective.

'He looked devilish,' said Norman, 'and another thing. He came very close to me.'

'Did he do that before?'

'Not as close as that, not as close as that.'

'I see,' said Sam, who did not see at all. What had this to do with anything? (You winking parrot, he thought fiercely.)

'How much will my ticket be?' he asked.

'Same as always,' said Norman, and laughed uproariously. 'Same as always.'

Sam threw a gaze of hatred after him as he made his

way to the nonsmoking saloon where he sat very up-right and watched a child making faces at him.

Devilish, he thought. Devilish. So Donnie was on the ferry after all. He hadn't been killed by Annie, of whom Sam was suspicious from the very beginning because her hair was shorter than the church of St. Paul strictly allowed.

When the ferry docked he strode over to the bus and sat in the back seat. He closed his eyes, feeling suddenly that his blood pressure was rising. He made a mental note that he must take more exercise. His contempt for the easy-going Highland way of life was beginning, he knew, to affect his health.

When he opened his eyes he was horrified to see straight ahead of him above the driver's head a screen on which there was a picture of a man and a woman in a naked embrace. For a moment he was worried that this was the content of his sinful mind, but when he looked about him he saw that the passengers were fol-lowing the film with interest.

Without thinking, he strode down the aisle and said to the driver, 'I want you to turn that filth off at once.'

The driver, manoeuvering equably between a foreign car and a truck, said, 'I can't do that sir. The passengers are watching it.'

'And I am not a passenger, then?'

The driver considered this, chewing gum all the while — he was in fact quite young, and he wore a uniform and a pair of boots from Macdonald and Sons — and then said, 'I suppose you are, in a manner of speaking.'

'What do you mean, in a manner of speaking?' said Sam loudly. He wanted to kill this young man, he wanted to wrench his bones apart, he wanted to spatter his blood all over the bus.

While he was standing there, a large man with a red face touched him lightly on the shoulder, 'Had you not better sit down, Papa? The rest of us can't see the screen.'

Sam turned round abruptly. He should really kick this man in the groin, but on the other hand reasoning might be better.

'This is pornographic filth,' he said. 'This man should be ashamed of showing it.'

'We like pornographic filth,' said the large man simply. 'Don't we?' and he turned to the other passengers. There was a chorus of 'yes'.

'You tell that bowler-hatted nyaff to sit down,' said a woman with red hair, who was sitting in one of the middle seats.

'You tell him to sit down or you will kick his balls in,' said a fat woman with a fat chin, who was sitting in the front seat.

'You sit there, Papa,' he said, 'We don't want to put you out.'

I will report that driver, thought Sam, in incoherent rage. I will report him and hope that he will be dismissed from his job and turned out on to the street of whatever town he lives in. I wish to see him starving and indigent, begging for food, subservient, humble, asking for mercy as the whip lashes his back.

He maintained a resentful silence till the bus pulled into the bus station at Inverness, imagining only the large man's flesh dripping from his bones in hell. He then got off the bus in the same silence, making a note, however, of its number. He should have slugged that bus driver, and that large man. He felt a familiar contempt: his toothache throbbed, his arthritis hurt, his blood pressure was rising, and now he felt a pain just above his heart.

When he was biting into the pie which he had bought at the café at the bus station, he belched. Thank God it wasn't his heart, it was indigestion. He looked around him savagely. The usual crowd of nonentities, fodder of the Clearances, remnants of the '45. He felt such unutterable contempt that he almost vomited on the spot. The good ones had gone to America and now he was left with illogical dross, who winked their eyes and seemed to have a secretive tradition which they would only tell after eons of time had elapsed. 'You should do something about your salt,' he said to the proprietor as he left, and felt the deep satisfaction which his parting shot had given.

The question however still remained. Had Donnie stayed in Inverness, or had he gone further afield? He felt a sudden pain in his kidneys and went into the lavatory at the side of the café. After he had finished he looked around him for a towel but there was none available.

'You use that machine over there,'said a young man with a grin.

Sam pushed the button on the machine but finding that no towel came out of it he left in the worst of humours.

What else could he do but parade the streets of Inverness.

If it hadn't been for that film he could have questioned the bus driver about Donnie Macleod. But he could not ask a pervert for information and in any case he would have lied to him. I have to assume that he is still in Inverness, he thought, there is nothing else that I can do. I have to rely on the intuition of the great detective. I feel in my bones that he is still here.

In comparison with Portree, Inverness was a metropolis. He counted ten churches before giving up: the Woolworths too was larger. Feeling tired, he sat down on a bench for a while. He took a blue tablet from his pocket and swallowed it; it should keep his thrombosis at bay.

A man who appeared to be a beggar came and asked him for money for a cup of tea.

'No, thank you,' said Sam. The beggar looked at him for a moment and then scuttled away.

Sam gazed straight ahead of him at what appeared to be a cinema, and whose lights flashed intermittently. A moment's thought however told him that it was not a cinema. It was in fact some kind of a club as he deduced from the large green letters which said "THE MESS OF POTTAGE". It suddenly seemed to him certain that he would find Donnie Macleod in there. He had no logical means of knowing this, only the mystical intuition of the great detective that he was.

He walked over to the building. Behind a glass screen sat a large woman who was wearing black lipstick.

'One ticket,' he said crisply. 'That will be enough.'

'Adult?' said the woman in a husky voice.

He disdained answering her; he had taken an instant dislike to her from the moment he saw her. But, more than that, he was suddenly struck by an intuition as he looked at her naked neck and almost naked breasts. He couldn't quite focus on what it was but it told him he had come to the right place.

He left the lobby and going through a door ahead he found himself in a large smoky room, in fact Sodom and Gomorrah. The noise was frightening. Dancers clung closely to each other. Some people were drinking at tables. On a stage a large, almost naked, woman was prancing. So this was what the Highlands had come to after the Clearances. So this was what the '45 had done to the people. So this was the result of the sheep runs and the deer forests.

If it hadn't been for his instinctive desire to pursue his investigations, he would have left at once. He touched his bowler hat as if for comfort.

As he stood there hesitating, a large woman wearing

red lipstick and tottering on the sharp heels of her shoes (Armstrong and Brothers, Inverness) came up to him and said in a deep attractive voice, 'Are you not dancing, darling?' And before he could say anything he was dragged into the maelstrom of light and noise.

'Where do you come from?' asked his partner, against whose naked breast Sam's bowler hat bobbed like a cork in a stormy sea. He couldn't account for his hatred of her, but said sharply, 'Portree.'

'Portree, darling. Over the sea to Skye and so on.' (Her cliché immediately offended him. Why, wherever one went nowadays, could one never get a really satisfactory religious discussion?) Her mouth yawned, surrounded by a red infernal line.

'Do you always wear a bowler hat when you are dancing?' she asked.

'Always,' said Sam.

'How flip, what an ironic comment you are making on our contemporary society,' said the large woman. 'You must be a satirist, rather like Juvenal.'

Not another pagan writer, thought Sam savagely. Why not one of the prophets such as Micah? But no one ever mentioned Micah or Jeremiah.

The large woman made as if to kiss Sam. He turned his head away from a breath that stank like garlic.

'Has "THE MESS OF POTTAGE" been here long? he forced himself to say, trying to wriggle away from her hand which rested on his rump. A thrill of horror pervaded him.

'Who knows, darling?' So many questions, so few answers.

Her shadowy chin bent over him and suddenly the solution to the case was as clear to him as a psalm book on a pew on a summer day. He withdrew rapidly from the woman's embrace and made his way to the exit, the sign for which hung green above his head.

'I knew it,' he said to the receptionist, 'I knew I had seen you before. The hair on your chest registered subconsciously.'

'It is true,' said Donnie. 'You have run me to ground. I suppose it was Annie who hired you...'

'It was indeed,' said Sam. (You ungrateful pervert, he muttered under his breath.) He wanted to crush Donnie into a pulp. So he had been right after all. That red spot beside the word 'enuff' had been lipstick, not blood.

'I couldn't stand it any longer,' the vicious serpent was saying. 'I was tired of hearing Leviticus and especially Numbers. You have no idea what it was like. If I had stayed I would have gone mad.' (You horrible atheist!) 'I couldn't distinguish between the Amalekites and the Philistines.' (You pathetic heretic!) 'When sitting at the table I would have an impulse to stab Annie with a knife. I knew there was no future for us. I saw this job in the paper and applied for it.' (You belly-crawling snake!)

So this was why Donnie had said to that ineffable boring ferryman, 'A change is good for a man.' So this was why he had looked devilish.

'I won't go back,' said Donnie simply, 'I'm happy here. I love my new dresses. Pink was always my favourite colour.'

'You used to dress up in your bedroom,' said Sam.

'How did you know that?'

Sam ignored the question. After a while, Donnie said, 'You are a marvellous detective, the best in Portree. But you can tell Annie I will not go back. I have made a new life for myself here, and Jim and I have fallen in love. Tell her that if it hadn't been Leviticus it would have been someone else.'

Sam Spaid looked into Donnie's blue eyes, thinking many thoughts. His gaze rested on the rose in his corsage. Then he sighed deeply. 'I think you are taking the wrong course,' he said. 'But I cannot take you back by force, much as I would like to. You will have to give me something in your handwriting that will show Annie that I met you.'

'Yes indeed,' said Donnie, taking a pen from his purse of tinselly yellow. He wrote rapidly, and Sam read what he had written.

'Annie, you're a good woman. Too good for me. I shall think of you as a sister.
Signed Deborah.'

'Deborah,' said Sam between his teeth.

'Yes, I have changed my name. Jim didn't like the name "Donnie".'

Sam put his hand out to Deborah (Donnie) while at the same time he was thinking that he should kick her(him) in the teeth.

'Goodbye,' he said. 'And may you learn more about those fleshpots than you know now.'

As he left "THE MESS OF POTTAGE" he was thinking that he would not make much from this case — his fee, and his expenses, which were the rates for the ferry and the bus.

He would have to try and find some more complicated cases. Little did he know that there was one waiting for him which would be known as "The Case of The Disappearing Pulpit" and which would push his logical powers to the limit, and bring him expenses to the devil-possessed village of Acharacle.

Murdo's Thoughts

Sometimes Murdo on a summer evening in the half-dark would say, 'Ah, you inscrutable panoply of stars, you mute procession of infinite diamonds, how little must our petty diurnal motions interest you. The Co-op for instance with its ancient till, the butcher's with its pendant flesh of sheep and swine, how little do these things rest on your individual stellar minds.

Galileo stared at you, so did Copernicus and Bruno. To the Greeks you were circles, to us you are misshapen ellipses. As Angus Macleod, dressed in his dungarees, makes his humble way to the sawmill, or Donald Munro, idle now for five years, switches on the television, while at the same time giving a howl of rancour and rage against the existential vagaries of his life, and especially his wife and his children, are you apprised of them? No, indeed, you are not?

And as I myself confront my typewriter and the sheet of blank paper which I have inserted there, are you aware of my baffled thoughts, and my envy of Catherine Cookson? I am sure you are not.

No, you continue on your luxurious orbit, you execute your perfect motions, you are perfectly happy to ignore us. And you are right to do so. For what are we but inferior notes, dwarfish monads, dressed in our various arrays against eternity.

When I was young I scampered lightheartedly

through fields of bluebells. The daisy was not alien to me, nor the crocus. The rhododendron rose up in all its glory and so did the forsythia and the chrysanthemum.

Now all is different. I find little to adore in the clematis or the philadelphus. What is the japonica to me, or the hydrangea? I find myself a pitiful object among these blooms. I limp among these vernal blossoms.

I am tired of the old names. I wish to invent new ones such as "Chrtex" or "Crymp" or "Haberdragon". I wish to say in the language of the spheres "Choro lem typsck." Gaelic is not enough for me, nor is English. I wish words composed entirely of vowels, such as "Aiuoiauo", or of consonants, such as "blxrnmst". On landscapes of such names I wish you to shine, O immortals.

And indeed you have shone for a long time. The dinosaur you have seen and the mastodon. You have seen the "q" and the "p" Celts. You have seen the Co-op, opened in 1924, with its many tins, its freezer, beans and spaghetti. Are you not tired of these sights? Are you not exhausted by fish fingers?

Our telescopes penetrate the atmosphere. But what indeed have we learned of ourselves? I ask you that and I know that you will not answer. Everything is old, yet everything is new or middle-aged. Saturn shines on a bald head, Pluto on a random beard or chin. A waistcoat here and there is lit up by Mercury. Denims are illuminated by Jupiter and kilts by the harsh skies of Mars.

Proud travellers of the sky — majestic yet not erudite voyagers of space — what shall you say of him, this worm, Murdo Macrae? Shall you say of him, he is a good man, potential author overwhelmed by failure; or on the contrary shall you say he is a squalid idler, who inhabits a squalid tenement? Shall you say, he is a bag of wind, a sporran full of fantasies, an infernal git, or do you indeed say, he is a valuable soul untainted by the millions of Vietnamese, Malaysians, Chinese, etc, bowed over their watery plots.

Is he a con-man, you ask, is he a florid vocabularist? Or is he a poor fool in the labyrinth around him?

It is sad that you are not able to speak, ancient though you are. It is matter for sorrow that you have not even learnt a few words of Gaelic in your voyagings through space. You are not even able to give the Gaelic for "satellite" or for "comet". And what do you say of "Arcturus"? If you could speak, what stories you would be able to tell. Of the '45, of the Clearances or kelp: of run rig, the sheiling and the genealogies of Ossian. Of Presbyterian conspiracies, and the plots of the Elect. Of the angst of Arnish and the euphoria of Eagleton.

But your silence remains as we turn from thatch to stone, from exchange to subsidies. You will not speak, you remain mum. You keep your stellar mouths shut, you refrain from gossip. You have nothing to say about Mary Nicolson's moustache, or the scandal associated with Dougie Cameron's blankets. You do not ask: why has David Shaw painted his window panes green or why does Lily Stevenson live entirely on corned-beef?

And we accept this because we must. We bow down to it, as we have no alternative.

To the lyrics abandoned in space we say "enough", and to your diamonds we say "sufficient".

I now have to return to my humble abode for a call of nature, asking myself indeed about the ambiguities and paradoxes of the word, and I leave you, masterful emblems, with these words: Remember the dead, O remember the dead, but remember the living more.'

Murdo as Poetry Critic

'Three of the greatest lines in the poetry of our people,'
Murdo would often say, 'are the following:

> *Shawbost is the most beautiful to me (lit. with me)*
> *where I was brought up when I was young*
> *where there are the peatstacks ....'*

I know that simple translation cannot give one the
melody of these lines, but it can tell us the content. I
admit that when I read these lines first I didn't understand their pathos, their heartbreaking directness. Peat-
stacks, I thought, what have they to do with the lyric,
with that dictum of Milton's about poetry being 'simple,
sensuous and passionate.'

However, as I re-read these lines, being brought up
directly against the 'peatstack', I thought — this is precisely is what the poet is trying to do, precisely this is
his aim. He is like Wordsworth presenting us with the
peatstack in all its bald thereness. It rises concretely
from the abstract (for Shawbost from a certain point of
view can be considered an abstract) and moreover it
does so in a vivid manner, as indeed the gum tree in all
its ghostliness arises from Australian poetry.

Furthermore, what else is being done here? The peat-stack is, as we all know, the source of heat in the islands. For many years we had no electricity, as we have now. The peatstack was what held us together as a story-telling community. It sustained our communal broodings. The poet encapsulates in the peatstack a whole way of life, communal aid, tractor, cup of tea, the indigenous and ambitious lark, the wounded landscape, the heather.

The poet in fact is bringing us up against the reality and glory of our lives. Out of the sensuous melody of the poem there rises like a historical monument, like a ship in the night, the peatstack. It casts a shadow, the shadow of history, and indeed that is its purpose.

I look forward to more of these brutal yet poetic invasions, as for instance "lazy bed", "HIDB" and "District Council". Human kind cannot bear much reality,' wrote T.S. Eliot, but I think they can. Only when this has been done can we see that we are mature, only then can we say with the great poet Walt Whitman, 'I suffered: I was there.'

Murdo's Random Jottings

A foot in both cramps.
Flogging a head nurse.
A snake in the grass keeps one on one's toes.
An apple a day keeps the orange away.
He left under a shroud.
No man is an island but Harris is.
Duty is only skin keep.
A stitch in nine saves time.
Thyme is of the essence.
A putter wouldn't melt in his mouth.
Sneaking about is the better part of valour.
Casting your Fred upon the waters.
It's all ill wind that does not recover.
Turning the other sheikh.
The tigers of luxury succumb to the warthogs of
    righteousness.
The herring volk — people of Peterhead.
My art's in the Highlands — Van Och.
A woman's place is in a home.
All that glitters is not lead.
There's no fire without smoke.
Incidents will happen.
Here be dragoons.
People in grass skirts shouldn't throw cinders.
If you can't stand the heat get out of the furnace.
The first shall be last and the last shall be fifth.
Sand Ahoy!
Never say Dai.
Helping a lame writer over his style.
Going to work on a leg.

MURDO'S PROPHECIES

- When the Access card is lost, there shall be sorrow in the glen.
- When the two cows meet head on at the Road of Fasting there shall be a dark bridge over the Navon.
- Whoever wears tartan that day shall not return till the fairies rise from their mounds.
- The Dark Woman will not eat the pebbles of repentance till Calum Mor loses five sheep.
- When there are three measures of snow a white man will descend to the trough.
- A fire in the thatch will cause the downfall of two dynasties.
- A ferry will be built on the bones of the last horse.
- The Macleods of Skye will submit to the papers from the far country.
- Whoever brings a polled cow to Innis nan Gall shall suffer for it.
- None shall inherit the House of the Green Chimney but the man with tackety boots.
- The man who sings through the nose will signal the downfall of the Mod.
- Pretend how he will, the man with the long kilt shall not be forgiven.
- The empty sporran shall be filled with the milk of mercy.

- The delinquent rabbit shall be cast on the dungheaps of history.
- On the day that the stranger is nigh, the milk bottles from the mainland shall fall over.
- The bell will cry 'Alas' when the robes shall fall from the statue.
- The end of the world is near when the MacBrayne's ship will be on time.

"The End of the Raj"

by Murdo

'It was evening,' wrote Murdo hurriedly, 'and the Raj was sitting in the sun. The last punkah had fallen silent, and the skulls of the Pathans hung against the clouds. Lady Robinson-Hattersley sipped her gin and tonic, her helmet tilted over her dark hair. She was sending her sons home to Folkestone again; how could she bear it? The heat was dazzling, the mountains in the distance were white, many men had died crossing that rope bridge: Champers had won the VC there.

Who would remember them when they were gone, the griff, the tiffin, the bhistri (the water carrier), the dhobi (or laundryman), the lowly mehtar (or sweeper)?

Not far away was where old "Nobby" had won the MC, and "Pillbox" the DSO. She felt her imperialist imperative weakening. This water was poisonous and the ayah had blisters on her chin. So much for the cholera that was sweeping the valleys.

Alexander had once passed this way. In his curt way he had killed many tribesmen. In the glimmering light she saw the thunderbox with her husband Willie sitting on it. He had a straw moustache and was wearing his topé. She thought, perhaps I should take a photograph of him for my book "Leaves of a Memsahib's Notebook", but she decided against it, for her husband was a great killer of snow leopards, bears, parakeets and orioles. He also hunted the warthog, that slow yet venomous inhabitant of a harsh landscape.

"Make sure you pack their iron beds," she shouted to the servant. And don't forget the fitting for the stiff upper lip. Inside, her tears rained down. The Dogras were waiting for her will to fail (she could hear their drums during the night), but she would not fail. She had met Willie on the boat coming out. He had said "Hm" twice before she noticed him. Then she had seen that he was indeed a white man, brave, though small. He had shown her photographs of mynahs, some of which were black. These are what we call coal mynahs, he had said. It was the only joke she had ever heard him make. He had a good "seat", none better. He was a sahib.

The tiger rug of which the children were so frightened seemed to move in the dim light. Poor Willie; should she shoot him or not? The house was full of dead birds and dead animals. Wherever she went she was tickled by feathers. Not a book in sight. She stretched luxuriously and yawned. The Union Jack fluttered over the kopje (no, that had been South Africa). To see Nanga Parat on a clear day was a delight. She would miss it. It looked like... like... soapsuds. She picked up the glass with "Northeastern Indian Railway" engraved on it. She was going to seed; she had given up wearing her spats.

She must get out, OUT, OUT. The smell of the goatskin irritated her. She had given up her polo. It annoyed her that not a single British family but had had an officer relative in India. So many VCs, MCs, and DSOs. As a child, before she had met Willie, she had been contented with her lot. But now she had India in her blood.

She saw Willie rising from the thunderbox. How she loathed him: it was only now that she recognised this at last. His monocle flashed in the last light of the Raj. His braces were the colour of the Union Jack. Behind him she saw a canna, the Kalaho peak, a markhor and a yak.

She must get home. She must make it to Essex once more. She must talk to the vicar. She put on a choga and a koi.

She took the rifle down from the stand. She would say that seeing him rise unexpectedly in the half light from the thunderbox, she had thought he was a Pathan or one of the dogras who eat the flesh of warthogs.

She sighted along the rifle — and fired. The Raj for her had come to an end. The Boxai Gumbaz rose up in front of her. Thunder echoed from the hills. The monsoon suddenly poured down.

"Will there be anything else?" said the bhistri.

"That will be all," she said in her husky voice. As she went in she muttered to herself the words:
"When you're wounded and left on Afghanistan plains
And the women come out to cut up what remains
Just roll to your rifle and blow out your brains
And go to your Gawd like a soldier."
Was it her imagination or was the tiger rug moving again?'

MURDO'S NOTICE FOR THE LOCAL NEWSPAPER

I was sorry to hear, wrote Murdo to the local paper, of the wedding of Finlay Thomson at the early age of 50.

Brought up in Crossbost, he was the only son of a crofter. He showed great promise at school, being especially good at plasticine, and eventually became a teacher.

In the 80s he was a fine exponent of parsing and analysis, and in the 90s he discovered Dickens and Tennyson.

For many years he lived in a room and kitchen in Glasgow. There he met Dolina Maclachlan, a Domestic Science teacher. Their courtship was spasmodic and various, and they would go to ceilidhs together.

I had many fruitful discussions with Finlay about grammar.

I shall remember him as a fine loyal friend, and one who would give the shirt off his back if it was absolutely necessary.

His many friends will regret his marriage. He was a generous host, a learned colleague and a first class grammarian. We shall not see his like again in much of a hurry.

Our sympathy goes out to his wife, the second daughter of Angus and Katag Maclachlan, 30 Main Street, Shawbost.

At the going down of the sun and in the morning we will remember him.

Murdo Macrae

A 'P' AND A 'Q' CELT

IN CONVERSATION, BY MURDO

On a puiet morning they met, Qeter Morrison and Qaul
Thomqson.

'Haqqy days,' said Qeter.

'And to you,' said Qaul.

The Qeewit was chirqing in a qoqlar, a qlumq monk was
qainting a manuscriqt.

'It is the pueer air that is in it,' sail Qaul after a qause.

Qrofound was the morning, and the qeasants at their toil,
heads bowed over their qotatoes.

A daqqled horse stood by a qost. A stream riqqled in the sun.

A puiq fell from Qaul's liqs.

'When did you last see the father?'

A smile dimqled Qeter's amqle face.

'We will need Qrior notice,' he said.

Puietly chuckling together they entered the qantry and then
the vestry, qassing a qaqal bull on the way.

Murdo & the Jehovah's Witness

Sometimes at breakfast time Murdo would say, 'Not to have been born is the best. Any more toast?'

'It is there beside you.'

'So it is indeed. Not many Highlanders would eat muesli. Stands the Co-op where it did?'

'I'll leave you the dishes,' Janet would say.

'Yes, indeed, I am an heir of infinite riches. Why don't we get a washing machine?'

'If you would sell one of your stories we might. I'll never know why you left the bank.'

'It was indeed mysterious. My head ached and a drowsy numbness dulled my senses. That was the long and short of it.'

When Janet had gone, he muttered to himself, that was indeed the long and short of it. Not many of us had the chance to do the work for which they were created. Thus a born poet becomes a bin-man and reads the *Financial Times*, while a violinist becomes a manager of sewage. How shall the soul be saved?

At that moment the doorbell rang.

'Who are you?' said Murdo, peering out into the mirk.

'I am a Jehovah's Witness.'

'He does indeed need a witness,' said Murdo, 'as he is invisible.'

'Do you know about Life?' said the Jehovah's Witness.

'Indeed I do,' said Murdo. 'I will not let you in, as the house is untidy. Are you selling your product?'

The Jehovah's Witness said, 'Have you come to the Cross? Are you washed in the blood of the Lamb?'

'Not that I am aware of,' said Murdo. 'Your product is not faring well these days. Tell me, is it the fault of your training? Do you need a sales manager? You must advertise on TV.'

'I would like to discuss the Bible with you,' said the Jehovah's Witness, wiping the rain from his glasses.

'I am sure you would,' said Murdo. 'But not all of us get what we want in this life of ours. Some of us have heard of Barth, Tillich, Kierkegaard. What do you say to that?'

'Listen,' said the Jehovah's Witness, 'it says here: "Blessed be those that hunger for they shall be filled".'

'The hunger is indeed there,' said Murdo. 'But nevertheless you are a corrupted man. Hie thee elsewhere. Mrs Davidson has no one to talk to but her cats. Speak to her. Take thyself hence and turn first right then left. What have I to do with thee? And may I say unto thee, what dost thou know about life, thou effete ventriloquist? It will not profit a man to be sneaking up and down and expecting his neighbour to give him cups of tea. Avaunt, thou boil on the face of the waters. Begone, thou imp of false theology. Were my ancestors Covenanters for this? Go and get thy coffee elsewhere.'

The Jehovah's Witness turned on his heel. Murdo put his head in his hands and stared for a moment at the gravel and the hills. It was a day on which the witches might have met Macbeth. His spirit was low, his angst was troubling him.

He washed and dried the dishes, muttering about Hades. Comfort me with asphodels, he said to himself.

He glared malevolently through the window at Mrs Macleod.

'Nymph, in all thy orisons be all my sins remembered,' he said. And then he said, 'I will not submit, never, never, never. I am of the proud clan of the Macraes. I will fight this metaphysical smirr on my own. Thank you.'

Seordag's Interview with the BBC, by Murdo

'How old am I? I am ninety-five years old. We used to have a black house, a dung heap, and a byre. Now we only have a microwave, a cooker and a freezer.

My daughter looks after me. She is seventy years old. She has arthritis, bronchitis, and a bit of heart trouble. I was never at a doctor in my life; I could leap the height of a trout over the house.

In the early days, we had brose, oatcakes and milk: now we have weetabix and sometimes my daughter makes lasagne.

The oral tradition? I remember that we used to sit around the fire in the ceilidh house reading *The Guns of Navarone* aloud. It took three weeks. Before that we had *Where Eagles Dare*.

I read the *Peoples Journal*. The other day I saw a funny thing in it. "Highlander in kilt wishes to meet another Highlander in kilt."

I listen to Scottish Dance Music as I am immune to it now, and it doesn't affect me.

I feel as young as when I was working in the run rig. I could go to a dance yet (laughs). My leg is as white as the bogcotton on the moor.

I had seven children. Most of them worked for the Gaelic BBC. Did you ever hear the programme "From the *Slabhraidh*"? It was my daughter Sheila that did that. It used to be on at four in the morning.

Of course when I was young we never locked our doors. Stealing was unknown. There was some incest, but if a man was caught stealing he would be put out of the community.

We have funny neighbours now, *a ghraidh*. A Frenchman, a German, and a man from Portugal. They are the only ones who speak Gaelic.

You have fine knees yourself, *a ghraidh*. It is a pity that I was not seventy years younger.

And of course there is not a cow or horse on the island now. The blacksmith's closed twenty years after the last horse died. Calum Macmillan was always a bit slow. I used to go up to the last horse and stroke him. I would give him a saccharine as we had no sugar in the war. Oh, he knew he was the last horse all right. It was like the second sight.

I never had the second sight myself, though my sister had. She prophesised when the first planning officer would come to the island.

There was a time when I was in Peterhead and Wick. I would be following the herring but it might not be the same herring.

My eyes are as sharp as ever. I can see a buzzard from five hundred yards and a proverb from further away than that.

Oh, I remember Cathy Morrison. She was very witty. She said to me once, "You are as fat as a barrel with a cran of herring in it." (Wipes her eyes, laughing.) Another time she said to me, "That man is as thin as a rake."

You've got nice soft knees. Sarah my daughter is in bed with the arthritis. Her husband's dead. His last words were, "It's the fine day that's in it." You're not to run away. I was only joking. Don't lift your voice like a seagull when the planting is being done. Come back. Come back. Come back.

I never told you about the *tairsgear.'*

THERE WAS A SHOULDER, A SURREALIST TALE, BY MURDO

Once upon a time there was a shoulder and it shouldered far away. Wherever a battle was to be found it was there. It was to be found in India, South Africa, the Sudan. It would wave the troops on, and the fine absent chiefs. And sometimes it would compose a pipe tune. This shoulder had not much to say for itself. It might go into a bar and ask for a half and a half. That was the maximum of its verbiage. It was the best-behaved shoulder in the British Army.

It never thought about the intricacies of things: it put itself to the wheel. And it would sometimes fight against shoulders of its own kind.

At one time it had tartan on it, then nothing at all, then tartan. The shoulder loved the tartan. It had a great reputation for strength.

One time it found itself at the Green Hills of Tyrol. It heard the cowbells and it felt at home. But then it saw other shoulders coming towards it and it began to snarl and then to fight. That is why there are many shoulders buried there.

This shoulder would cast a shadow over a burnt house. Sometimes it would brood about the oral tradition, even when the foreign officer was shouting, 'The first duty of a shoulder is to die for the King or the Queen, as the case may be. Failing these, an attaché will do.'

When the shoulder returned home there was no sign of its village. It wept and wept for a long time. Then it was given a home help and sat in a chair watching TV.

Sometimes, if it was in a good mood, it would say, 'When I was a shoulder in Afghanistan,' or it would say, ' That was where I got my campaign medal. It is as pretty as a rainbow.'

All the shoulders from the Highland regiments asked for their own minister. They were very upright and honourable. They had been brought up on the very pith of buttermilk and were very strong.

None of the shoulders ever rode a horse and none of them became an officer.

If it wasn't for these shoulders where would the British Empire be today?

It's a thought, isn't it?

THE STORY OF MAJOR M^c CARTWRIGHT, BY MURDO

Major Terence Cartwright, wrote Murdo, was an interesting man. He came originally from Hampshire.

When he arrived in the small Highland village of A....... his first act was to learn Gaelic. Most of the natives had long ago given up speaking Gaelic but Major Cartwright was determined to keep the old traditions alive. He dressed in the kilt, made crowdie, cut the peats, and had a little dog called Maggie. The dog looked like a dishcloth which you might see on a kitchen table.

At ceilidhs Major Cartwright would introduce the singers and the songs.

'Tha mi toilichte a bhith an seo an nochd,' he would say, speaking with great aplomb. He would insist on speaking Gaelic throughout the ceilidh, though the natives were not used to it.

'We should not let these Sassenachs run our affairs,' he would say, when he spoke English. He voted Scottish Nationalist at all times and would say, 'It is high time we had a government of our own.'

He loved cutting the peats. Everyone else hated doing them: all of them used electricity, gas or coal. But to Major Cartwright cutting peats was the bee's knees. He was never happier than when he was out on the moor among the larks and the midges.

'A fine figure of a man,' the natives would say at first.

The Major made oatcakes, which the natives despised. He would hold his little dog in his arms and speak to it in the Gaelic. It looked like the bottom of a mop.

'*Tha mi uamhasach toilichte,*' he would say. A few of the natives initially disliked him: then more and more as they saw what he was up to. 'Anyone would think we were living in the eighteenth century, he is bad for our image.'

He advertised lessons in Gaelic but no one went. He wanted to teach the natives the correct use of the dative and the genitive, but they would have none of it. He even began to write poetry in Gaelic, which he published in a national magazine.

'Many is the time,' he would write, 'that I would look over to Harris of the lazybeds. It was there that I was reared.'

The natives thought that they ought to get rid of him. They felt he was riding roughshod over them. His poodle was stolen and Sam Spaid was asked to investigate. Sam Spaid hated the Major at first sight and would only speak to him in English. He found the poodle on a washing line: Anna Maciver, who was eighty years old and almost blind, had hung him there.

'You senile idiot,' said Sam Spaid under his breath. 'You incontinent oaf.' He was wearing a black suit (from Anderson and Sons) and a pair of black shoes (from the Co-op).

'Here is your... thing back,' he said to the Major. (You imperialist hound.) The Major made crooning Gaelic noises to the dog, based on a lullaby from Iona.

'What are the marks on my dear Maggie?' said the Major.

'Pegs,' said Sam Spaid curtly.

Sam Spaid went off in a rage to his next case. He had been paid in oatcakes.

The Major began to make oatcakes and crowdie for

sale, but no one would buy them. He felt that he was becoming more and more unpopular.

At night, on his own, he read *Dwelly's Dictionary*. He knew the Gaelic for the birds and trees and flowers, shellfish, and so on. Most of the Gaelic speakers from the village had joined the Gaelic Department of the BBC.

The Major had never been so lonely in his life, not even on Salisbury Plain. His wife had stayed in Hampshire and wrote to him in English. He replied in Gaelic. It was with great difficulty that he had managed to take the poodle with him.

'I did not find anywhere more beautiful,' wrote the Major. 'The lochs, the sheilings, the streams.'

He picked up his bagpipes and began to play the "Lament for the Children." In the distance he would hear the music from the disco: and someone singing "Walk Tall" in an American accent.

It was one of his great sorrows that he could not find the Gaelic for "poodle".

Night fell over A.... . The Major put away his pipes. What had he done wrong? Whenever an Englishman came to the village he would say to him, 'This is not for you. You have done enough harm. Do you know for instance the Gaelic for "rhododendron"?'

The Englishman took the hint. After a while no one stopped in the village, and the bed and breakfast trade failed.

There were murmurings of discontent, rising to open roars of hatred.

'I was born in Uist of the peewit and the rowan,' wrote the Major. The moon shone over *Dwelly's Dictionary*.

One day with his poodle he left. All that was found in his house were some oatcakes, some buttermilk and some crowdie.

He went back to his wife in Hampshire.

Often he would look back on his days in A... with stunned amazement. He changed his poodle's name from Maggie to Algernon.

'We have seen much together,' he would say to him. 'The time is not yet. The books at the airports are all the same.'

He gave up the bagpipes and gave his kilt to Oxfam's.

He and his wife opened a restaurant in Hampshire. His oatcakes, buttermilk and herring became famous. The menus were in Gaelic with English translations.

In the evening of his days he would say, 'Fine it was for me that I dwelt once in Harris.' An Indian was chewing his oatcakes with the air of a gourmet and a South Korean was delicately sipping his buttermilk.

'Fine it was for me,' he said, 'that I tasted the salt herring in my youth.'

Some Jottings, by Murdo

1) Imphm
   Hem
   Alas
   Och
   Alack
   Er
   Rrm   *(Preferential treatment)*
   Um   *(Friendly fire)*
   Ahem   *(Salutary suggestion)*
   Em   *(Categorical imperative)*
              (The rule of the proletariat)
   Arrum   *(White heat of the technological*
              revolution)
              (Aesthetic, ethical, existential)
   Hum   *(Expanding universe, big bang,*
              quasar)

2) And then my heart with pleasure grinths
   and dances with the hyacinths.
                    (Murdo Wordsworth)

3) It never came a wink too soon
   nor brought too long a day
   but now I often wish the night
   had sung a roundelay.
                    (Murdo the Hood)

4) For a' that an' a' that,
   the microwave an' a' that
   the man o' independent mind
   is king o' men for a' that.
   (Murdo Burns)

5) There lived a wife of Usher's Well
   and a wealthy wife was she,
   her cooker was of the deep deep clay
   and her fridge was ivory.
   (Murdo Ballad)

6) Never never never never never
   never never never never never.
   (Murdo Shakespeare)

7) Come into the garden, Mod,
   for the adjudicator has flown.
   (Murdo Lord Tennyson)

Sam Spaid

Sam Spaid bent down and picked up his mail from the lobby. He was in his blue and white striped pyjamas (Co-op, Portree) and his blue slippers (Anderson and Son). There were only two pieces of mail: one a communication from Strathclyde, which he crumpled into a ball and threw into the bin, the other an envelope with his name but no address written on it. And no stamp.

He opened it. There was a piece of paper inside it and written on the paper in shaky handwriting, which at first he found difficult to decipher, were the words 'You slimy inauthentic theologian'. Immediately his face contorted with fury, red spots danced in front of his eyes. He read the words again then looked at the paper and envelope, searching for clues. But there were none. He did not recognise the handwriting.

As he ate his muesli, he studied the message again. Who could have written him that letter? He didn't think there was anyone who disliked him, unless it was one of the criminals he had uncovered in his many successful cases. His tea tasted foul and so did the toast.

Apart from the Case of the Disappointed Evangelist he had nothing on his plate. 'Inauthentic', eh? Not many people would know that word. It must have been an educated man who had written that note, and there weren't many educated people in Portree. Most of them were actually working for the Gaelic Department of the BBC and therefore not at home. Furthermore, the criminal had delivered the letter himself, the filthy horrible swine, riff-raff left behind at the time of the emigrations.

He sat at his desk all day drinking glass after glass of water and studying the handwriting. He thought he had seen it before but could not identify it.

That night he read three chapters of Numbers before falling into a deep sleep. In the morning he found another envelope on the floor (there were no other letters) and when he opened it he read the words: 'You ineffable religious snot. Why don't you look under your pillow?' The handwriting was the same, and still not easily read.

Under the pillow he found an old digestive biscuit. He stared at it in amazement. What did this mean? His large face reddened and boiled with rage like a choleric crab. His hand tightened on the toaster. Who was trying to get at him? He, who had never harmed anyone in his life. He took out the list of his cases filed for future publication:

The Case of the Highland Horror (that was that woman Miss D. Lennox who had inherited a haunted castle from her stepfather and who had been found dead in a rain barrel).

The Case of the Enchanted Elder (that had taken him to a strip tease club in Oban and lavish fees and expenses).

The Case of the Australian Cousin (who had easily been uncovered, because after twenty years in the outback he still spoke with a strong Highland accent), and many others. He could see no obvious clue there. He had a sudden idea. Getting hold of a piece of wood he nailed up the letter-box.

The rest of the day he spent simmering quietly, now and again thinking of throwing a plate or two at the wall, but with great difficulty he refrained.

He read two more chapters of Numbers that night before falling asleep. In the morning he went confidently into the lobby. In spite of his confidence there was an envelope there. He opened it and read the fateful words: 'You futile investigatory excrescence. Look under the teapot.' And there he found a squashed pancake, one of the ones he had bought from the Co-op.

His mind staggered under the weight of the puzzle with which he was confronted. He felt giddy. First his arthritis, then his heart bothered him, but there was no one to whom he could recount his symptoms. He did not wish to go out, though he thought of himself as a popular man who always had a single word for everyone. His usual swear words 'Clearance fodder' and 'imperialistic poodles' fell flat from his lips. Nor was he much better pleased with his recent invention 'Black house perverts'.

The day passed in a stupor of surrealistic scenes and images. He cut himself when opening his usual tin of corn-beef; his malignant flare at Mrs Macleod was only a shadow of its former ferocity. He looked through all his correspondence to see if he could find the handwriting. But all he could find were old letters. One of them began: 'No, you ineffable stream of pee, of course I can't marry you. Do you think I'm a masochist?' (That was from Marjory.)

Another said: 'I send you by return of post a copy of *The Triumph of the Elect*, which you sent me. Please defray postage.' (That was Evelyn.)

There was also a letter from the Income Tax which asked him for a list of fees and expenses. It was addressed to Private Eye Sam Spaid, Portree, Isle of Skye.

Finally, there was a letter from the local Police Department querying his interrogative techniques.

But he did not find the handwriting he was looking for.

He could not work like this. That morning he had put on a red tie with a brown suit, and he had broken two cups.

An idea came to him. He would stay up all night, but he would have to make sure that he did not fall asleep.

He chose from his extensive library a book called *The Amusements of the Prophets*, and read avidly. It must have been at three in the morning, and when he had reached the part about the honey, that his left hand began to twitch violently. He stared down at it in surprise. Then he began to move, as if under an obscure order, and found a piece of paper on which he wrote the words: 'You eccentric Moabite. Look under the money jar.'

He went to the cupboard and took out a doughnut, which he placed under the jar. He put the paper in an envelope and laid it on the lobby floor, then wrote his name on the envelope. All this time he was in a state of suspended animation.

So it was himself who had written the messages after all. He put away *The Amusements of the Prophets*, carefully marking down the page. One thing bothered him. Why had he not recognised his own handwriting?

Then the answer came clear to him. He had written with his left hand. Flooded by childish memories mixed with bile, he remembered that when young he had written with his left hand. Then his grandfather, a vision of a long snot-infested beard and small hating eyes, had hit him repeatedly with a belt till he had changed hands.

All was now clear to him. He went to his file and wrote the Case of the Blur-lined Letter.

Then he sank to his bed and slept till midday when a stunning but perplexed fisherman introduced him to the Case of the Docile Drifter.

THE CONCIENTIOUS PARTNERS

J. D. Williams and Oxendales, wrote Murdo, were great heroes in Highland mythology. It was from them that coats, pillowslips, frocks, etc, came by mail order and, generally speaking, COD.

Many was the time that One-eyed Angus, the postman, brought such a parcel to a house. Angus would only give the parcel to the addressee and to no one else, no matter how closely related. Thus he would make his way to the peatstack or to the cornfield or to the seashore, in order to deliver the parcel which might in fact be a wardrobe or sideboard. In this fashion people would have to carry large or small sums of money with them at all times in case One-eyed Angus loomed over the horizon with a parcel. He was a small man with a red face, and no knowledge of Berkeley or logical atomism at all.

'Much as J. D. Williams and Oxendales are great Highland heroes,' he would say, 'and much as they are handsome as the oak-tree, slender as the salmon, with eyes as blue as the egg of a peewit, however their hearths are open to the stranger, and however kind they are with venison, wine and mutton, they are causing me no end of bother. Plus,' he said, 'receipts are difficult to obtain when there is heavy rain in it or a violent snowstorm.'

Poor Angus, ignorant of philosophy or theology, inhabitant of a land of clouds and thistles, lone struggler through the world of the COD! It is often I think of him resting his wardrobe in the land of true hospitality and curiosity, himself untainted by alien materialism, for he was too poor himself to afford such luxuries. He would mutter 'rich bastards,' as he trudged through a marsh and the birds were singing cheerfully overhead.

For he was consumed by his Presbyterian conscience. 'No, indeed,' he would say, 'I will not give this parcel to you, though you may indeed be the mother or the brother of the acc......., the addressee.'

And therefore the largesses of J.D. Williams and Oxendales would cause One-eyed Angus to froth at the mouth. 'These men,' he would say, 'heroes though they are for their munificence, have caused more chilblains than anyone else; they have bowed my back and made my hair the colour of the bogcotton. I would be glad if small articles were sent for.'

And so it was that this happened. People felt sorry for One-eyed Angus and stopped sending for wardrobes, dressers, etc. Nor did these great heroes ever discover why their trade with that area declined and diminished. Little did they realise that it arose from the community spirit of a village and the Presbyterian conscience of one man. For how indeed were they likely to know of it, but it warms our hearts to think of it.

Now Angus rests under the daisies by the sweet water of Loch Gair. Above his head waves the simple daffodil, but of a winter's night if you are passing and happen to shout the words 'J.D. Williams' or 'Oxendales', a figure will suddenly arise, putting on its boots, and with a face contorted with rage in the eerie light of the moon, will appear also to take a bag and trudge through mud and marsh to cornstack and peatstack, muttering to himself over and over 'Bloody COD,' — and a hand grained with toil, will stretch out for the fateful wardrobe, or whatever, and sign in the moonlight the paper which One-eyed Angus holds out.

MURDO'S PLEA
FOR A NATIONAL ANTHEM

Sir,

I would like to show you why my song, 'There was a Shoulder', should be considered as our National Anthem and therefore fit to be sung at rugby, lacrosse and hockey matches, whenever two or three or eleven are gathered together.

The arguments in favour of my song are as follows:

Firstly, everyone has a shoulder. This is a very important point. It means that instead of being divisive or contemptuous or bellicose, it draws attention to what we have in common, e.g. a shoulder. There is no aggression here, only the cry of suffering humanity, for there is no one who does not have a shoulder.

Secondly, and following from this, there is no reason why the two teams should not sing my anthem. Neither would be betraying nationalistic fervour, etc, in doing so. They would be learning about our common humanity, its hopes and fears, etc, and the mutual kinship of shoulders. Indeed also the shoulders of each member of the team could be bared at this point.

Finally there is a pathos there which could appeal to all men of goodwill. This Scottish shoulder wandering freely all over the world — where does it come from, where does it go to? Is it an orphan, a refugee? Who will look after it, who will give it shelter? Our thoughts go with it. It draws attention to our solitary state, our need for friends. It belongs to the category of *sunt lacrimae rerum* as seen in Virgil, Tennyson, Larkin, etc.

I hope these thoughts will be of use in this troubling matter, and in this troubling time. I refer of course to Beirut.

Yours etc,

Murdo Macrae

Murdo on Translation

Sir,

Can any of your readers help me? I would like to translate the following passage into Gaelic for a book I am writing, The Thing in Itself: A History of Sofas from a Philosophical Standpoint.

Here is the passage:

'Now Köhler said, "You see two visual realities." As opposed to what? To interpreting presumably. How does he do this? (i.e. how is this established?) It won't do to ask people. Köhler never says it will but he says, "If you're not blinded by theory you'll admit that there are two visual realities." But of course he can't mean only that those who don't hold a certain theory will say, "There are two visual realities." He must intend to say that whether or not you're (1) blinded by theory, or (2) whether or not you do say one thing or the other, you must be right to say "there are two visual realities".'

Yours in anticipation,
Murdo Macrae

PS Does Cogito ergo sum, mean, I think, therefore I add up?

DETERIORATION IN SAM SPAID

A great change came over Sam Spaid after the Case of the Blur-lined Letters. He became a more private eye than before. He trailed people only halfheartedly: his witty sayings became fewer: he dressed in a sloppier fashion.

He asked himself the question, 'What am I doing? What is the meaning of my work? Do I do it for honour? Yes, perhaps. Or for the conscience of mankind? Again, perhaps.

'These days and nights of snooping in doorways, beating people up and being beaten up, these hours of sitting outside the Co-op disguised as a crofter or an insurance agent, what are they for?

'Am I in fact a crusader or a knight or an Old Testament prophet? I have burrowed into bins and learned that all fish is gross. And that tinkling symbols can be found among slimy sandwiches.

'When I was young I snooped with innocent assurance. I shadowed people without regret. Now however I ask myself, Why, Why, WHY? Do I deserve the title "private eye" and what does it mean? Is it a pun on "private I" or have I touched an optic nerve?

'And was the meaning of the letters revealing that I was spying on myself?

'When I was young I always thought that this would be my *metier*. I spied and snooped on both my parents. One night I looked into their bedroom and, the horror, I did not recognise either of them. From that night I decided to find out who these people were, *and what that thing was for.*

'I dreamed of unearthly secrets, of being paid for scavenging about. Cases of theft and incest abounded, though, thank God, I have not found any necrophily yet. Fearlessly, I strode the street. "That is the private eye," the people would say. I was in the public eye. A private eye in the public eye! That was a paradox which caused me many a wry smile.

'Now my innocence is gone. The words, "If it were not so I would have told you," come often to my mind.

'Last night the answer came to me. It was simple and clear. I shall change "private eye" to "scourge of God." A fiery cloud will go before me at night and a cloud shaped like a waterspout by day. I shall strike out of the whirlwind. I shall accept the sacrifice of sheep, my nostrils shall smell the fat of the roasting oxen. I see sin everywhere, for example a "syndrome", i.e. "an airport for sinners" and I leave you to deduce what "syncope" means.

'My whip is upon you, ye Levites: and my lashes upon you, O ye Philistines. You will not be free of my finger-printing, O ye Moabites. I shall pursue you to the fourth or fifth generation, for I am Sam Spaid, erstwhile "private eye" now "scourge of God."

'And this change shall be made on my stationery.' Thus spake Sam Spaid.

THE SCOTTISH
DETECTIVE STORY, BY MURDO

The howdumdeid was leeing on the flair when Inspector Macdermott arrived.

'Hoo is he ca'd?' he speired the hoosekeeper.

'The Rev. M. Kailyard,' she said.

Her een were a keethin' sicht.

The Inspector peeked through the winnock. He saw a shelty, a quey, an' a watergaw.

'Did aebody ca' on him?' he speired.

The eemis stane was leein' by the corp. The Inspector keeked at his watch.

It was ane after ane.

'Ay' said the hoosekeeper. 'He had a lang beard an' he faced baith weys.'

'Baith weys,' said the Inspector, gantin'. The draff o' last nicht was dowie in his mooth.

'He was ca'd Anti — somthing.'

'Aunti something?'

'Ay.'

The hoosekeeper wis a drodlich. Forfochen, the Inspector picked up a caird frae the flair aside the howdumdeid.

His chouks fell.

Professor Anti-zygygy, it said.

The Inspector faddomed it a' noo. It was a liteerary maitter. A' to dae wi' dialectic an' the contradeections. He reca'd whit the hoosekeeper had said.

He was facin' baith weys. That was eet. Frae Byron

tae the present day.

'*Sunt lacrimae rerum,*' he said. 'Git Professor Anti-zygy-gy. There is bluid on the eemis stane.'

'Seil of yir face,' he said to the hoosekeeper. 'An' dree your weird.' Then he clamb intae his carr.

'There's a fine look tae the lift,' he said to a passing farmer.

'Na, I dinna want a lift,' said the farmer.

'Ignorant knoul — taed krang,' said the Inspector to himself, as he drave on.

Murdo's Ballad

There lived a wife o' Usher's Well
an' a wealthy wife was she.
Her mooth was o' the bad bad clay
and her dress was crammasie.

'To Noroway to Noroway
to Noroway o'er the faim.'
Thus spak the wife o' Usher's Well
who was a canty dame.

She hadna sailed a league, a league,
a league but barely three
when the canty wife o' Usher's Well
went a' tapsalteerie.

Gie tae me a hame help, she said,
a hame help but barely seeven
afore I climb that heich heich wa;
until the gates o heeven.

They brocht unto her a hame help
a hame help but barely twa
and she didna climb tae the gates of heeven
but she played at the ba.

An' lappit in her bedclaithes fine
she asked for her barely bree
'For my three sons are in the the brine
and i'm fair drowkit,' said she.

FRAGMENT OF A PLAY
BY MURDO

(Set in a Chinese restaurant. Low lights, black phone, etc.)

Enter Yu Fuang: Is the chowmein ready yet?

        (pause)

Lin Fang (his grandmother) soliloquises:
> The moon over the Yangtse.
> When shall I see you again? In my
> pigtails, wandering near the Gate of the
> Beetle in the year of the Dragon...

        (enter Angus)

Angus: *A bheil an chowmein deiseil fhathast?*[1]

Yu Fuang: *Cha bhi e fada.*[2]

        (pause)

Lin Fang: ...The Emperor riding past.
                 Dust by the Gate of the Beetle.

Angus: *Agus king's prawn.* [3]

Yu Fuang: *Ceart* [4]

        (pause)

Yu Fuang soliloquises: I wish my honourable granny
                 would help me. She soliloquises all day.
                 In this so honourable alien land I feel
                 so tired, so tired...

        (pause)

Voice outside the window sings:

> The town hall clock in Stornoway
> chimes its message every day...

Lin Fang:
> That so honourable young voice
> recalls to me a poem by Li Po:
> On the Yangtse with a glass in my hand
> and looking at the moon
> I think of Peking...

Angus:
> *Tuilleadh rice.* [5]

Yo Fuang:
> *Ceart.* [6]

(pause)

> I long for Confucius.
> The Flea Church is strict, strict...

(pause)

Angus:
> *Agus 'sweet and sour.'* [7]

(pause)

Ling Fang:
> Honourable young man has hit nail on
> head. Sweet and sour is how I feel far
> from the land of my so honourable and
> psychologically correct ancestors.
> I think of Li Po:
> The Emperor has exiled me here
> to the Island of Hoo Pung
> I look at the moon...

[1]   *Is the chowmein ready yet?*
[2]   *It won't be long.*
[3]   *And king's prawn.*
[4]   *Right.*
[5]   *More rice.*
[6]   *Right.*
[7]   *And 'sweet and sour.'*

FURTHER THOUGHTS OF MURDO

On a fine summer's day as he sat in his study, Murdo would see the road in front of him and people passing up and down on it as if on their way to Camelot or Ballachulish. Beyond the road was the heathery sward, on which his eye would rest lovingly, and he would think some such thoughts as these:

It is indeed fortunate that I live here where, at the first hint of spring, the humble crocus peeps out its lovely head as it nestles, perhaps beside a helpful stone. The ill-clad buzzard perches on a post and the rabbit plays his innocent games. The seagull makes a flying visit and the innocent tit gobbles up the guilty worm.

In the autumn the tree burnishes its leaves and in the winter a cloak of snow descends. Sometimes a cloud passes overhead and I ask myself, where is it going on its innocent way? Is it perhaps heading for Sumeria where the alphabet was first invented, or to Egypt where the pyramids were erected by many men and where the innocent cat was worshipped, or perhaps to Carthage where the innocent Dido burnt herself after she was deserted by the con-man Aeneas, and of which city it was said, 'Carthago delenda est'.

Night falls, and the patient owl goes 'Tu whit tu whoo,' and the beetle drags his weary length along. On such a night did Juliet in her native Italian speak sweet nothings to Romeo, and in Latin also did Caesar whisper in Cleopatra's ear, 'Te amo,' — that great man who had Pompey decapitated and who said, '*Veni, vidi, vici*' when he landed in Britain.

Then in the month of March the daffodil rises proudly from the sod and later still the rhododendron. In this fruitful land however we do not have the gum tree, nor does the melon or the kiwi fruit flourish here. The orange nor the tamarind grows easily, nor the breadfruit tree, and the palm tree only takes a passing interest.

Time passes slowly, and during the harvest the mouse nibbles at the golden blades. The crooked scythe is no longer to be seen, but the reaper is: and instead of the upstanding horse we have the tractor slaving eagerly on behalf of mankind. Such is progress at this present moment in time. The future is uncertain and the past is the past.

No longer is it the case that we have the corncrake, for poisonous and venomous substances have put an end to him, and the lark is not feeling so well. The raven no longer comes to the winnock and the common dove is sickening. What has happened to the crow and the swallow? They will all go the way of the roc and the auk and the dodo. The domestic hen too is in danger, and the flagrant goose.

Life is changing and things are no longer as they were. Where are the summers of our childhood when we would paddle in the burns, and catch the seemly trout.and the salmon which was not safe from us. They are, I fear, no more.

Some such thoughts as these would stir in Murdo's mind as he looked out of his winnock and saw two or three council employees now and again cutting the grass, and a big black dog with slavering jaws would trot along on some mysterious quest of his own.

Murdo in Conversation

Sometimes Murdo would stop a smallish farmer and, like the Ancient Mariner, hold him in his thrall. He would speak to him in the following wise:

'If a man says to me looking at the sky, "I think it will rain therefore I exist," I do not understand him.'

But more importantly he would discuss things which interested the farmer. Thus he might say, 'The Highlander never looked kindly on the pig. Is this perhaps because he belongs to one of the lost tribes of Israel, as is commonly said; for you may see many domestic animals in the Highlands, including the dog and the cat and the sheep, but never the pig in its pink splendour, though he is mentioned in the tale of the Prodigal Son.

'Also, at one time, the Highlander used to drink the milk of the ewe and, in extremis, he would take blood from his cow, mix it with oatmeal and make a meal of the resulting melange. That was at the time of the Clearances.

'The innocent and cud-chewing cow the Highlander has taken to. It reflects from its eyes his own leisurely concerns, his hopes and fears, etc. These eyes are, as it were, treasuries of oral tradition and language. The tup too he has taken to and the ewe, known as the yowe in the areas where Lallans is spoken.

'But the pig, never the pig. Something in the pig disconcerts him and at the same time repels him. What can that be? Is it perhaps something to do with its cannibalism, reminding him of the days of the clans? The goat he will accept with its capricious leaps but not, not, the pig.'

Murdo would end with the following quotation:

' "What is the use of studying philosophy if all that it does for you is to enable you to talk with some plausibility about some abstruse question of logic, etc, and if it does not improve your thinking about the important questions of every day".'

And as an illustration of this, Murdo would quote:

' "It would have made as little sense for me to say, Now I am seeing it as... as to say at the sight of a knife and fork, Now I am seeing that as a knife and fork".'

'Good-day to you, sir.'

NEIGHBOURS

Murdo hated the programme *Neighbours* and when it came on he would start screaming, or go into epileptic fits. Catalepsy too was one of the strategies that he employed. If none of these was available he would say, 'This is the end of civilisation as we cobbers know it.'

Or, more simply, 'We will roo this.'

Or, 'Rolf Harris' impudent didgeridoo will replace the psaltery.'

He would hide in sheds or in wardrobes or under beds, or pull blankets over his ears. His nervous system would appear to collapse and he would mutter frenziedly some such word as pommy, or emu.

Swag, billycan and eucalyptus would become to him common swear words, and so would billabong. 'Speak not to me of sheep stations,' he would say, 'nor tickle me with the didgeridoo.'

It would take hours before, with the help of valium, he would settle down again in the arms of his loving sheila, Janet, who would whisper to him over and over, as if to a sleeping child whose limbs have run wild, 'It is fine and dinkum. See you later. Bad Rolf Harris will not get you nor does the billabong await you.'

THE WHIST DRIVE

A very nice whist drive was held in our village the other day, *(wrote Murdo for the local newspaper.)* Mrs A. Macleod held her cards very well and Mr R. Macleod was everything that was required. There was no rancour between Mr and Mrs D. Macleod, though in fact Mrs D. Macleod missed a trick or two. The matter, however, was smoothed over amicably.

Tea and cakes were purveyed at the interval. These were of the highest quality. Mr F. Macleod was in sparkling form: his quips were of a rare vintage. Mr Z. Macleod told the story of the Angels of Mons once again.

When the whist was resumed after the fine tea (for which we must thank Mrs G. Macleod) everything was as nice as before. Mr F. Macleod allowed himself a few pleasantries, and I wish you all had been there to hear them. Mr N. Macleod and Mrs G. Macleod shared a joke.

Much work goes on behind the scenes at an event of this kind. We wish to thank Mr L. Macleod for setting out the chairs so nicely: Mr K. Macleod (known to his friends as Kenny) for handling the raffle tickets so well:

and Mrs S. Macleod for donating prizes which were won so handsomely by the recipients, who came forward so nicely and with such humility.

Murdo Macrae

(NB. I would like on behalf of the Committee to thank our local writer Mr Murdo Macrae for writing so nicely about our event.

Mr W. Macleod)

(And finally I would like to thank Mr W. Macleod for his able words about Mr Murdo Macrae.

Mr T. Macleod)

POEM BY MURDO

I remember, I remember,
the house where I was born.
There never came a Saturday
but Mrs Macleod came in at morn.

She never brought a thing to us
but she would say 'An ounce
of sugar is what I would like' -
These words she would pronounce.

And then my mother, bless her heart,
who is long in the ground,
would say 'I will not give you an ounce
but I will give a pound.'

And O the smile upon the face
of the cunning A. Macleod.
'I hope I'm not a wink too soon.'
Her heart was beating loud,

as she would say 'O welladay
I'd like your phone to use'

which then my mother would reply,
'Whatever's mine is yours.'

And then alack such looks so black
got Anne from old and young
as she went on, for ages long,
with her repulsive tongue.

Alack alack and welladay
such looks from old and young
and instead of the phone a thick thick rope
about her neck was hung.

Mirror of Magistrates

(A little play penned by Murdo Macrae)

Mary:	And what was the North Sea oilrig like, this time?
	(pause)
Norman:	Bad. Bad. (*removing his diver's suit.*)
Mary:	And were you reading that pornography again?
Norman:	Yes, Mary, I was.
	(pause)
	I was so alone. So alone.
	(pause)
	Alone.
Mary:	Was not my photograph good enough for you?
Norman:	It was different, different.
	(pause)
	Different.
Mary:	I'm going to divorce you, I made up my mind.
	(pause)
Norman:	This is a big blow, Mary, no denying it, it's a big blow for a man just home from the oilrig.

	(pause)
	Have you given it long and hard conseederation?
	(pause)
Mary:	Yes, I have. I am tired, tired.
	(pause)
	Tired.
Norman:	You will have to help me, Mary. There was nothing to do but look at the sea. You have no idea, no idea. It was driving me mad, mad. It was my pornography saved me.
Mary:	Saved you?
	(Knock on the door. Enter Anne Macleod.)
Anne:	Could I borrow an ounce of butter, Mary?
	(Mary and Norman burst out laughing, and are soon in each other's arms. Normality in the shape of A. Macleod has brought catharsis.)
Mary:	Butter! Butter!
Norman:	Butter!
	(They go off into hysterics again. Curtain slowly falls.)

MURDO & THE
DETECTIVE STORY

As Murdo, relaxing his labours, would watch the TV in the evening, he would say to the weather man when he had finished, 'Thank you very much.'

If a play was on he would say, 'Watch out. There is a villain behind you.' Or, 'I am sure he is from Control. It's either MI4, MI5, MI6 or N2, or WST 8. How can anyone know? We are not privy to such information.'

The advertisements he took as part of the play. 'Ah,' he would say, 'I now see the connection between the story and the Heinz. It was inevitable.'

He would also at various points quote proverbs such as the following: 'There's many a slip when you are sitting on the fence.' Or, 'Thank heaven for small little girls.'

He would imitate Sherlock Holmes' facial twitch and say to Janet, 'The game's afoot.' Or, 'I would refer you to my little monograph on scythes.' Or, he would go around for days saying, 'You know my methods.'

For instance, if an insurance man came to the door selling insurance, or a retired mendicant schoolteacher selling double glazing, or a stranger who was looking for a house in the village, he would say to him, quietly, 'You know my methods.'

He would sometimes write to his daughter Mary, who was at Glasgow University, in the following way:

> 'My dear daughter (or Hastings as you are better known),

I wish to say to you Sacre bleu. Or, a thousand thunders. Or, C'est curieux, n'est ce pas. Or some such words.

Eh bien. I hope that all goes well with you and that you are in le bon heart. You are indeed an exotic creature. Depechons vous, Hastings, we must keep this to ourselves.

Your devoted father,
Murdo Macrae.

Mary was quite used to such letters and would often reply.

Dear Mr Poirot,

After much doubt and indecision, I am at last emboldened to write to you. I have to tell you, that after every meal I eat in this house I am as sick as a chien. I fear therefore that I am being poisoned.

There is a train that arrives here at 1.01. If you are not on it, I fear that you will not receive another letter from me.

(Ms) Shirley Wainwright, M.A. PH.D.

Murdo would reply,

Dear Miss Wainwright,

There is no stamp on your letter. I therefore cannot take it seriously, I the great Poirot. Sacre bleu!

Yours,
Hercule Poirot.

Dear Mr Poirot, (Mary would answer)

I am at the moment imprisoned in an attic, bound hand and foot, apart unaccountably for my right hand. Unaccountably a pen has been left beside me. I have thrown this letter out to the milkman (I think I am somewhere in East Sussex).

Yours sincerely,

(Ms) Shirley Wainwright, M.A., Ph.D., N.U.T.

And so on.

There were many programmes that Murdo didn't like, including ...., ..., ..., ..., ..., ..., ..., and ...., etc.

There was one games show master whom he hated, and he would shout at him in a frenzy, 'You slimy snake. You snail of the first water. You tongue of newt.' At such moments he would froth at the mouth, then say to Janet, 'I shall be all right in a few minutes. You go out and enjoy yourself. I need no attention from anybody. In my day we gave all that we earned to our parents. I know that I sacrificed myself for you but you are young, you need fresh air and so on. Leave the tablets beside my bed.'

And so on.

He also hated programmes about the Arts, Science, Religion, Philosophy, Politics, etc. He was never happier than when he was watching a detective story on the television. Locked-room murders were his favourites followed closely by carnage of any kind.

If the murder was set in Mexico he would say to Janet, 'This will be no good.' But if it was set in a country house, cut off by snow or typhoon from civilisation, the telephone lines down and the microwave not working, he was deliriously happy. His favourite line was,

'And where were you at 11.03 last night?'

followed closely by,

'I devoutly hope that we will be in time, Watson.'

He loved fogs, masks, disguises, cabs, men who had known each other in Australia, or Indians who slouched round standing stones or pubs.

In bed one night he said to Janet,

'The dog didn't bark.'

'I didn't hear it,' said Janet.

'That is precisely the problem,' he said, and went to sleep.

He suspected that films had deteriorated rapidly once people began to talk on them and that the thriller had destroyed the detective story.

'Look what we have lost,' he would say, 'great lines such as these':

"So it was not he who left the ball on the stair."

Or,

"Sometimes I feel I understand Anataxis, Nori."

'Ah, those were the days,' he would say to Janet. 'En vérité, these were the days, mon ami. Sacre Bleu!'

MURDO'S CROSSWORD

1		2
3		

Across: 1 Pshaw (3)

　　　　　 3 Nothing:　Central Heating (3)

　　　　　　　　　　　　　　 (reversed).

Down: 1 Part of Loch Lomond (3)

　　　　 2 Nothing! Cold! H　! (rev.) (3)

Solution: Across: 1 Och

　　　　　　　　　 3 HCO

　　　　　　 Down: 1 Och

　　　　　　　　　 2 HCO

Bring Me My Caber of Burning Gold

'The origins of the Highland Games', wrote Murdo, 'are lost in the mists of antiquity.

'All we know is that before a battle a number of little girls, usually dressed in tartan, danced the sword dance. Whether this was designed to perplex the enemy, we simply have no idea.

'Nor do we know whether there was a MacCabre clan. It may be of course that the word 'macabre' is a corruption of such a clan name, though again we cannot be sure.

'Whether the sporran was worn in battle is another enigma. It would seem that there would be no need for carrying money on a battlefield especially as after the battle there would be plenty of sporran searchers about, but again we have no certain information.

'The customs of the Highlands are indeed matter for deliberation. Why for instance is shortbread so dominant in our culture? One nation may have Beethoven and Mozart, another Michaelangelo and da Vinci, yet another Voltaire — but we have shortbread.

'The Second Sight is a troubling matter; so is the Oral Tradition. At this time apparently a certain house was selected in a village and all the villagers converged on it. There they would take part in their Oral Tradition till the early hours of the morning. We do not know (1) why this particular house was chosen, (2) whether the guests brought their own provisions, or (3) what the host thought of being kept up till all hours.

'Standing Stones are another mystery. Were they in fact a method of measuring the time before the Highlanders had clocks? Were they primitive sorts of rockets? Were they used for human sacrifice and did they cease when the Old Age Pension came into being? Some consider that they were used to identify Saturn, others suggest Mercury, or Jupiter or Harris: and yet others opine that they could locate quasars and pulsars, so intricate was their organisation. Traces of radio communications have been found at their bases, according to some amateur scientists.

'Further questions are: Why were these large stones hauled for miles and miles to sit beside this particular tea-room and museum? Why did these dwarfish beings (for these men were smaller than us) go to such inordinate lengths to build such a circle? Here they are coming from all directions carrying their colossal stones on wheelbarrows, mayhap having a little worthless conversation on the way, and perhaps on their arrival a glass of orangeade at the adjacent restaurant. It is a strange sight indeed. Science will have to advance much further in my opinion before solutions to these questions can be found.

'Other customs too are puzzling. Why do so many islanders wink with the left eye when they are talking? Does this indicate a period perhaps after the '45, when there were many spies in the Highlands? And why do so many women borrow sugar? Does this point to an age of deprivation?

'As I have written elsewhere, the role of J.D. Williams and Oxendales will also have to be investigated.

'Questions abound: for example, why is the Bible carried to the pulpit by an elder? Why do so many singers, even the most prominent, sing through their noses?

(And what does the singer have to say to the pianist before they begin their recitation?) Why does a fiddle group never smile? And so on.

'It can be seen that much remains to be done before we can get a true picture of our Highland ethos before we can sit down and say that these and no other are our mores, before we can discover who we muscular, brave, fair-haired and generous people, as it were, are.

THE KILT COMPLEX

According to Freud, the 'Kilt complex' originated in the Highlands of Scotland. He describes two kinds of personalities, the anal and the exhibitionist, as being prone to this neurosis. (The open-thighed is a variant of the second of these.)

The kilt complex, according to Freud, is closely connected with freedom. It is a reaction to the strict mores of the Highlander, and suggests clean-limbed ferocity connected with mountains and lochs.

The sporran may have originated as a container for the 5d and a counterbalance to the super-ego.

Outsiders, that is, people extraneous to the Highlands, may adopt this complex in order to be on the winning side or simply as a protest against the paucity of Gaelic in their chosen areas.

It may be noted that the longer the kilt the more neurosis it covers: one whose kilt almost sweeps the floor is liable to be a raving psychopath. On the other hand a short kilt suggests a free personality, one who might say, in Gaelic, 'My anima is my own to command.'

PS 'Kilty party' is known in the Highlands of Scotland as a ceilidh.

THE ROLE OF B&B IN HIGHLAND CULTURE, BY MURDO

This is a short monograph on the cultural role of Bed and Breakfast in our culture.

In the first place many landlords and landladies are able to take advantage of the (accidental) birth of a famous poet in the general area of their houses.

Thus they might say, 'This is where the noted poet Neil McEwan was born. It was quite close to my bathroom or bedroom that he wrote his most famous poem, or sat staring into space wrestling with the Muse. Not far from my living-room is where he died, at the early age of fifty-six. As you will see, my house, called in Gaelic the House of the Three Mists, is named after one of his most famous poems. My husband and I are great admirers of his work, and have been, since we moved into this highly competitive area. Many critics of his work have had bed and breakfast with us and have been, as you will see from the guest book, well satisfied with their accommodation, which is, as you will notice, en suite, though smoking is not allowed. There is ample evidence that Neil McEwan himself did not smoke.'

Thus landlords and landladies unselfishly advertise many of our most famous poets and artistes and sometimes do this by means of menus as for example the Neil McEwan soufflé, or venison à la Neil McEwan, or the Neil McEwan sorbet. Other literary references are the Neil McEwan Nature Trail, or How to Become a

Poet in the Neil McEwan chalet, or our Neil McEwan Blue Room. There is also Neil McEwan shortbread, or the Neil McEwan tie and scarf, or Neil McEwan toffee.

'It is indeed a happy accident that he was born and died so close to us. McEwans of course have lived here from time immemorial, though he was the only one up to his time to put pen to paper. His wife was from this area, and it is said that his famous poem to her was written when he saw her coming from the Co-op with the messages. His biro can still be found in his tiny study. He did not, as far as is known, correct much of his work, but relied on what he called his inspiration. Discarded poems were placed in a bin positioned where our kitchen now is.

'He had a wife and four children, none of whom followed him in his worship of the Muse. One became a bank manager, one became a doctor, one became a primary teacher, and the last one became a fish farmer. It is said that none of his family read poetry, not even their father's. He died without making a will while in touch with the Muse at that gate over there and on which you will see the notice: "Neil McEwan in touch with the Muse."

'It is said that he had a fight with a bard from a neighbouring village over some onomatopoeia and shouted to him, after knocking him down, "This fist is in payment for your metre."

'Copies of this book are sold in the foyer. Others can be obtained from the Neil McEwan Cultural Centre along with maps of his house. The Neil McEwan taxi service is also very useful, or you may stand on a wet day at the Neil McEwan Bus Shelter.'

Such are the many ways in which the literary qualities of famous poets can be promulgated to make their works and lives known to the passing tourist.

A POEM BY MURDO

The Isle of Lamis is of isles the fairest,
the smell of sphagnum is of the smells the rarest,
its heathery slopes where the pear resideth,
as also where the haughty deer abideth.

Many were the emigrants who went by train
to Glasgow City where there was not much gain
and some would say Alack and some Ochone,
as arthritis they suffered to the very bone.

Many was the time, when I was reared,
that the nest of the peewit was by me cleared,
or barefooted in the evening gloam
I would make my cheerful way home.

My mother's face I still remember yet,
her name was Anne (her sister's name was Bet)
and granny would be lying in her bed.
The oral tradition filled her grey-haired head.

I shall return from Glasgow by the train
and meet my youthful comrades once again
and we will talk about the days of yore
when never in a house was shut the door.

Murdo's Menu

¤   Clear Soup à la Oral Tradition

¤   Emigrant Haddock (with selection of sauces)

¤   Duncan Ban Macintyre's Braised Steak (with selection of carrots)

¤   Robert Bruce's Banana Split

¤   Sir Walter Scott's Meringue Glacé

¤   John Knox's Ice Cream Sundae

¤   Coffee, Tea, Whey, extra.

THE Teacher's
Farewell by Murdo

Friends and Colleagues,

Many thanks first of all for the small token of esteem you have given me — this excellent radio — and may I say that though I live a good few miles from the main road up, as you know, an isolated rocky track, you are most cordially invited to drop in and listen to programmes on this radio, though, as you may know, my own interest is Radio Three.

You ask me what I shall be doing with my time. I shall, I think, continue with my monograph on 'The Imperative Mood and the Roman Legion, a study in the Command', an area which has not been investigated in the past.

At this time too I might say a few words, as is usual on these occasions, on the future of Education. For my own department there is no future. It is, as you know, going to be a storehouse for videos. It will hear no more of the ablative absolute or the subjunctive.

When I came here first we had what were known as lines. Pupils were lined up as in a military posture. I don't know if you remember Miss Oates, a twittery sort of lady who collapsed on, as it were, the parade ground. Our Rector at that time known as Caligula — the doughty Mr Robb, M.A. — wouldn't allow her to be moved till the parade was over. After all, he said, that is what she joined the teaching profession for. Miss Oates taught Cookery, Domestic Science as it is known now. She was called, I think, the Scone.

Which brings me to nicknames. There was a Deputy Head known as Pompey. When it was discovered that Caesar had cut off the head of the popular general, someone must have envisaged Caesar saying, 'Pompey is only a deputy head now.'

I myself was known as Galloping Cicero, and there was a lady known as the Sliding Snake. She is, alas, dead as well.

We no longer of course wear the toga as we were wont, and that, I think, is a retrograde step. As someone once said — I hope the ladies present will excuse me — when we wear the toga, no one can say that our flies are open. The Romans were a wise race. If I may venture a little joke, one can say, there were no flies on the Romans.

Strange things happen in teaching. Once when I was walking to school — you all know that the motor was alien to me — a young man, an employee of the council, jumped out of a hole in the road that he had been helping to dig and thrusting out a dirty hand at me said, 'If it weren't for you, Mr Summers, I wouldn't be where I am today.' Such is life! And then of course there was Mr Greene who ran off with the coffee money. And Mr Hogg, who built his private fortune on the sale of the little pencils at the back of the EIS diary.

I loved teaching. What else might I do? What else could I do? I had the responsibility for moulding the minds of the young. Give me, I used to say, a perfectly empty head and I shall fill it with the dative, the ablative absolute, and the vocative case.

The Romans, of course, were not fond of jokes. When you are building an empire you can't be joking continually. And we must not of course forget that they had aquaducts as well. And the Ides of March.

It will be a sad day when we will not be able to translate the school motto from the original Latin into the colloquial version. Strength through Boredom. And indeed boredom is a weapon that we must not under-estimate. If we were not bored, would we have invented the fire, or indeed a grammar system? The world in my opinion has been propelled forward by boredom and that is why we pay attention to agreement of case and gender and so on. Thus the more boredom there is in a school the better. Was it not because he was bored that Julius Caesar sailed to Britain and said the famous words, '*Veni vidi vici*', which are an example of alliteration. (*Et tu Brute*, is an example of the dying fall.) But enough of that. For myself my days of teaching are over. I will go out into a world which knows not Horace, and meet, as it were, my landlady Miss A. Jones for the first time. I will see her as she really is, a representative of the common unclassical woman, ignorant, diffuse, but withal having a rough truth about her. I will listen to her trenchant descriptions and her illuminating stories — not indeed about Horatius and the Bridge — but that will not matter. For I ask myself sometimes in my moments of doubt, Did Zeus indeed make love to a swan, or did he come down to Danae in a shower of gold? Miss Jones would say 'No' and in her simple way she might be right. What is Dido's pyre to Miss Jones or Miss Jones to Dido's pyre? For her motto is, if I may venture a little joke: '*Mince sana in corpore sano*' and that is enough for her.

And so I say farewell to you all or, as I might put it, *Ave atque vale*. I say to you, keep the flag of boredom flying. Do not give in to the siren voices which whisper Munn and Dunning, or Standard Grade. And above all avoid those who speak of relevance. Relevance has never been important in education. I myself have never heard anyone speak Latin, saying for instance, 'Did you hear the weather forecast today?' or 'Keep on your own side of the road, you nyaff,' — but that does not perturb me. Indeed it drives me to greater efforts. For I hear the sound of trumpets in the words, 'The Rhine having been crossed, and the dispositions having been made, Caesar at his earliest convenience engaged with Pompey, who having been wakened from sleep, saw Caesar's forces drawn up against him, to his great astonishment.'

Such are the words of the classics and they should set an example to us all.

(Mr Summers sat down to prolonged applause and then exited, carrying his radio, having delighted everyone in the atrium, and having delivered himself of a sapient oration.)

Murdo's Letter to a Friend

If it were not so, I would have told you, and as it is I will not tell you. Such are the constraints of secrecy.

That is why I will not tell you what I had not meant to tell you in the first place. This letter is to inform you of my position and as it were to reinforce it.

You will I am sure not put me in the position of being forced to tell you something that if it were so in the first place I would not have told you precisely anyway.

I am sorry that this is so, but it is a result of integrity on my part and ignorance on yours. The man who does not know anything cannot be betrayed or betray.

Such is indeed the reason for this hasty scrawl against the pressure of events — a communication and an explanation. A presence and as it were an absence.

Our friendship will I am sure endure in spite of this contretemps.

With kindest regards and best wishes and I hope your wife is well.

> *Your true friend,*
> *Murdo Macrae.*

Murdo's Defence of the Pun

There are a number of people, (wrote Murdo), People usually of a Calvinist stamp, that is, ones who wear tight waistcoats and who have gravestone faces, who look down on the pun.

For myself, I believe this is a mistaken attitude and arises from jealousy and rancour on their part.

Shakespeare, for instance, the well known playwright, though his life is for the most part a mystery (we cannot even be sure of his portrait) used the pun a great deal, especially for characters who spent most of their time in woods or forests near Athens. Also Hamlet, though a tragic figure, was accustomed to use the pun. Thus, for instance, he said to Claudius, "I am too much i' the sun", which is a good example of a pun. How he managed to pun when so many people were being killed or committing suicide or drinking poison from cups in which unions (another pun) were thrown, we shall never know, but I think this shows the importance of the pun to Hamlet's psychology. Though, of course, other figures of speech were also used by Shakespeare, such as antonomasia, metonymy, synecdoche, onomatopoeia, not to mention the humble metaphor and the simple simile.

Another example is, "a little more than kin and less than kind". If a man of Hamlet's propensity for tragedy — a character based as it were on *The Spanish Tragedy* — if such a man, I say, uses the pun extensively, who are we to gainsay him? And there are indeed examples of the miching mallecho of people who never used the pun, such as Malvolio and Polonius, etc, etc. The taste for the pun in Shakespeare's tragedies is different from the lack of the pun in Greek tragedies, but that was because the latter (a) were translated by Gilbert Murray and (b) were religious. In any case when a man marries his mother, as happens in Sophocles, an opportunity for the pun is not often available. It would be laughable if it were.

Aeschylus too, as far as my reading goes, did not often use the pun. However, the pun is rife in Shakespeare. It is only such people as Sir Andrew Aguecheek who find it difficult to comprehend the pun.

It therefore behoves all those who assail the pun to be silent or to ask themselves why Shakespeare, whom I may call the noblest Roman of them all, used it so often, as indeed when Hamlet says to Polonius, 'It were a brute part of him to kill so capital a calf there' (punning, as you will remember, on the words 'Brutus' and 'Capitol').

'In my opinion only such people as bear a grudge against the world, people who appear to have indigestion, and also ones whose faces are as fixed as solidified dung, disdain the pun, even when used by a great Dane like Hamlet. For myself, I said to someone only the other day (it happened to be a day of almost complete silence), 'You could hear a pun drop', and later I added, 'You could hear a pan drop', which, in my opinion, though not as good as Shakespeare, does put a different complexion on, as Kant would say, the thing in itself: and is not bad for a Highlander who, as it were, wishes to undermine ideology and annihilate mores, and who sometimes, as it were, takes off on linguistic wing over the meagre county of ethics.

Murdo Addresses His Reflection

At times Murdo would address his reflection in the mirror in the following words:

Who are you, my exact reproduction, to speak so scornfully of precisely those people who are for the most part protecting themselves with tattered raincoats against the trenchant gales of Reality.

Do you not also have your clichés, your pallid examples or antonomasia, your limping metaphors?

And, after all, what are you but a writer who cannot write, a failure, as the world judges you, a pimple on the face of reality (though many questions are begged by such a word, especially since the electron was discovered).

And of course I am not ignorant of Freud, Jung, Adler and others whom I do not know about.

It is a problem, I might say a dilemma, which satirists of my stamp face. People will say, "Who is he? I kent his faither!" (as indeed they might have said of Oedipus or of the Saviour himself) and this shows the democratic language of the Scots, though the word 'kent' is, if I may interpolate, cause for ambiguity. However, facts are chiels that winna ding.

I, however, answer that I write as the spirit moves me, not out of hostility but out of joy: and that if any lame dog wishes to help me with my style he has my phone number.

It is actually to the Pharisees and a little to the Sadducees that my words are addressed. I wish to say, as Cromwell said to the Rump, "Pray in your bowels that you may think yourselves mistaken."

And so, perturbed spirit, which enacts my unshaven image, and as it were, hypocrite reader, I say, I have taken on board your point about clichés, and how we all need them: mankind cannot bear much reality (with my reservations about electrons, etc) and I would only say, I do these things out of charity. I have always disliked a tinkling symbol and speak directly to you in the name of Love who vaunteth not, and abideth with her two friends, Faith and Hope, in these, as it were, meagre pages of mine.

Murdo's Letter to
Mr A Macleod, 16 Park St, S...

Dear Mr Macleod,

You will not know me: I picked your name and address from
the phone book this morning.

I am at the moment engaged in a project on Happiness, and I
have selected you as one who might help me.

The first question I would like to ask you is: are you happy?
In answering this question, you might think of such things
as rate of inflation, mortgage, marital quarrels, your income,
your next-door neighbours, the number of your children, your
in-laws, your garden, number of rooms in your house,
whether you have a garage, distance from shopping centre,
money left over after essentials such as whisky and cigarettes
have been bought, etc. This is only a short list: others I am
sure will readily spring to mind, such as insurance,
subsidence, etc. However, when all these questions have been
, as it were, mentally catalogued and analysed (for this
progress is nothing if not scientific) I wish you to write down
a simple Yes or No in the box provided. Impressionistic ideas
are of no use to me: what I require is a scientific evaluation,
after all the factors have been taken into account.

When considering this question you might also ask yourself:
Do I wish to get up this morning? Do I wish to shave? Do I

*wish to howl like a wolf when certain persons are talking to
me? Do I wish to exchange a simple greeting in the morning,
or, on the contrary, do I wish to say, 'Why don't you go back
home, you newt' or eft as the case may be? Do I make faces
at myself in the mirror? Do I wish to commit suicide by
means of gun/sword/washing powder/gas, etc? If any of these
apply please have no hesitation in putting them down.*

*Then ask yourself this simple question, When I leave the
house in the morning, do I wish to return to it?*

*There are many instances of men, apparently perfectly
balanced, who suddenly and as it were on the spur of the
moment drive off to Inverness and are never seen again,
submerging themselves in the teeming millions. Ask yourself
if you are one of them.*

*Other instances come to mind, such as the man who went
berserk in the supermarket. One moment he was perfectly
sane, just like you or me, the next he was throwing cans of
dog food about indiscriminately. The mind is indeed deep and
mountains high. Such instances are well documented and
have occurred.*

*Then again you might ask yourself whether you are irritated
by minor things, e.g. if there is a traffic hold-up lasting three
hours on your way to the office, or if your wife coughs
persistently throughout the night so that you can't sleep, or if
the phone rings and when you answer there is NO ONE
there. Many such instances abound.*

*Remember, I wish you to write a simple Yes or No in the box
provided, but only after due consideration. If you find that
you can't answer, simply write, I find myself unable to
answer. Shallow judgements are of no use to me, as, e.g. after
a good meal, you might write Yes. It is the long haul that is
important. You may take days, weeks or even months to
answer. You may, if you wish, consult Schopenhauer in order
to make up your mind. Or you might ask a close friend or*

neighbour to help you. The main thing is that the answer should be scientific.

I look forward to hearing from you. And remember you are not alone. I am getting in touch with many other people as well.

And good luck and good hunting.

> *Yours, etc,*
>
> *Murdo Macrae*

Two Poems by Murdo

(sent to *Encounter* but returned)

(1)
When I was young and happy,
I heard a wise man say,
you cannot be a spendthrift
on very little pay.

But now I'm old and withered
I wish that I had known
that the cold winds of Rannoch
will howl about the bone.

(2)
When you and I were young, Maggie,
when you and I were young
the words of an old tradition
flew easily from your tongue.

But now that you are old dear
and wear a thermal vest
the sun goes down at evening
and love itself has rest.

Murdo at the Unemployment Bureau

Murdo carefully took off his black hat when he entered the unemployment office.

'Sir,' he said, 'I am not here to look for a job. I am here to help you. You are unable to tell me that Dante had a job other than writing poetry and the same is true of Virgil, Horace and other dagoes one could name.'

The man who was bending over the desk with a pen in his hand looked up at him in surprise.

'Indeed,' continued Murdo, 'it surprises me that a man of your largeness of mind, not to say diligence, should be working at all. A man whose job it is to give other people jobs is in my opinion an example of a paradox. There's too much of it altogether, altogether,' he added earnestly, while beating steadily on the floor with his right boot as if he were hearing distant music such as that made by a chanter.

'It would be much simpler if, as a man with a job yourself, you ensured that others had no work. You, sir, should be a barrier there preventing men from getting at machines instead of encouraging them, for machines have done a lot of harm in the world. I should be glad if you were able to tell me that there is no work available for me.'

The man raised his eyes from the pad on which he had been writing and gazed blankly at Murdo.

'In my opinion,' said the latter, 'you should, like a Roman emperor, turn your thumb down when a man comes for a job. You should be able to say that there are more men in the world than there are jobs to fill, for if it were not so how should we have governments and bureaucrats who are examples of people who have jobs yet do nothing. Isn't a bureaucrat an example of a man for whom a job is not available, though he works just the same? When one considers the world in this light, a simplification takes place,' he added, leaning forward and speaking rapidly while clicking his teeth at the same time. 'There was a time when there were fewer men than there were jobs. That would have been, I think, in the Neolithic Age or thereabout. But as time passed there was a great acceleration of men so that they passed the number of jobs available. Thus the mysterious thing has happened that since there are not enough jobs an absence of jobs has been created. Thus a bureaucrat is an example of a man who sits in a chair and gives others the jobs that he has not got. Similarly a critic is an example of a man who believes that he has a job, though in truth he has not. And one could enumerate other examples if one had the time.'

Before the man could answer, Murdo continued: 'I have given this considerable thought, and I think your job now is to realise the realities of the situation and say frankly that you have no job to give anyone, except an illusory job that does not in fact exist, and that instead of putting a sign up in your office and in your window saying that such and such a job is available, you should on the contrary put up a notice saying—

"IN THE INTERESTS OF REALITY I HAVE TO SAY THAT THERE ARE NO JOBS AVAILABLE AND THIS SITUATION WILL LAST AS LONG AS I AM IN THIS POST. IN OTHER WORDS IT WOULD HAVE BEEN BETTER FOR YOU IF YOU HAD NOT BEEN BORN".

'Do you not think, sir, that this is the greatest job that you can render the community, to tell them the truth that the world has run out of jobs because of the great increase in the number of people. There are of course jobs imaginable which you do not have and which society cannot afford to support, such as, for example, Grape Carrier to Patients in Hospital, or the job of Exposing Everyone in the Community in the Service of the Truth, but for the moment we shall not be concerned with them. After all, what did a melodeon player do before the melodeon was invented?' he said, poking the man in the forehead with the umbrella he was carrying, though in fact it was a hot dry day. 'I have come to wish you well in the loneliness of your command and to ensure that you will not betray the principles of injustice by offering anyone a job, for by so doing you would be continuing an evil which it is time we put a stop to, eradicated, wiped out, smashed.' And his voice rose in a terrible rage.

'Please excuse me, sir, for that outburst, but this is something that I feel very strongly about. For in any case what job could you offer me that would satisfy the huge spaces of my imagination? Have you ever considered that Plato evicted us from his kingdom, though he was nothing but a rotten dirty Greek with no proper religion? Now I should say to you that as there are no jobs commensurate with our imagination − I am talking about painters, writers, and so on − what would be the point of you offering me a job for telling such a bitter truth?

'Sir,' he went on, 'when one considers the mind and its limits, when you consider what you are and what I am, it might very well be that it should be I that is offering you a job, or even taking over from you, and relieving you of these metaphysical conundrums that you are subject to each day. Sir, it is with pain that I regard you and your trembling hands. For how can you come here every day knowing that you are taking part in a fraud: a seller and trafficker in jobs that do not really exist but which you have invented in order to keep civilisation going, such as for instance a Professor of Philosophy, or a Prime Minister. I submit, sir, that you have begun at the wrong end. Learn inhumanity, sir, offer the men to the jobs instead of the jobs to the men, for in that you will be in touch with the essentially contradictory nature of Christianity itself. Need I say more to a man of your obvious intelligence?

'And one final word before you offer me the job that I do not in actuality want, since it does not in fact exist, I would plead with you to have a slot system in which you do not have the titles of jobs but on the contrary the names of men, so that as the jobs appear they come in search of the men; I mean real true genuine jobs, jobs of a high class of reality. Think of me as a job looking for a man, and please believe me that as such I feel my own reality and also feel for you. Be hard, sir, send the men away and keep the jobs in the silence of the night and admire them as you admire the ideas of that rotten Greek Plato who had no real religion. Love them as they wish to be loved, all those lonely jobs, even those that aren't yet in existence but are, as it were, waiting in the aisles and the theatres of the absurd. And if you would kindly put some money in this box which would sponsor the creation of a Missionary Society to Bearsden, I would be very grateful. Humanity must be smashed, sir, eradicated, and jobs created in its place and given their rightful position and status in the world.'

After a while Murdo was aware that the man was looking at him with a stunned gaze while simultaneously his hands were trembling, and before going out of the door he said, 'See, your hands are trembling. That is a sign of the inconsistencies of the system which your subconscious is aware of, though it hasn't yet reached your conscious. I am sorry for you, sir, deeply sorry, and if it weren't that I see too deeply I would accept a job myself and even take over yours. Pray for us all and especially for yourself. We all have much to answer for, much to answer for.'

Gibbering mildly to himself he left the office, unfurling his umbrella to the hot dry rays of the sun.

MURDO'S POETRY READINGS

Murdo's first poetry reading occurred in a public bar, the organisers having decided to bring poetry to the people. The pub was full at the time — which was two o'clock in the afternoon — and as Murdo stood up, his knees trembling, the barman was shouting. 'Two pints and two martinis over there.' Murdo could not be sure afterwards that anyone in the bar heard him, though he had read the most metrical of his poems: the only result of his visit being that a small man in a cap had tried to borrow five pounds from him in the lavatory.

He was then asked to read at a small village hall in the Highlands. When the time for the poetry reading came there was no one there at all: and the lady that was in charge of the proceedings was nervous because she had forgotten to put up the posters. When Murdo, the first to arrive, went to the room where the reading was to take place he was going to be charged a pound by the door-keeper till he told her who he was. Eventually five people arrived, and after Murdo had read his poem "The Herring Girls" there was a spirited discussion about fish.

However, Murdo began to receive more and more invitations. His technique at any poetry reading was first of all to find out how much money he was to receive: and thereafter to wrap himself in impenetrable mystery. He spoke slowly and with great deliberation, sometimes explaining references which were entirely clear while leaving obscurities as they were. Thus he might spend a great deal of time on why he had used a simple place name, while he wouldn't translate some such word as '*duilgheadas*', for he often interpolated Gaelic words among his English on the analogy of Pound and Eliot doing the same with Greek and Chinese. On one occasion a member of the audience asked him an unexpected question: 'Do you feel you are a poet when you get up in the morning?'

After a long pause Murdo said, 'No, I feel like a prose writer.' He added, 'Non-fiction.'

When he stayed at his host's house, Murdo kept up the same impenetrable reserve. He also did some odd things. For instance he might take the bulb from the lamp and leave it lying on the table. Or he might face a picture to the wall. Or sometimes he would write a meaningless poem and leave the pages hanging in the wardrobe. He might suddenly say to the host, 'Whisky has the emotive yellowness of atrophy.'

Sometimes too, in order to give the impression of an intense insomniac, he would pull the lavatory chain several times through the night. 'I have an old malady,' he would say darkly, 'which afflicts me especially at three in the morning.'

Another interesting ploy was to leave the company of the host, shouting, 'I've got it,' and rush off to his room. Then he would sit on the bed smoking for an hour and arrive later as if nothing had happened. All this gained him a reputation for mysterious genius.

His great difficulty was with his smoking. Most times he would find there was no ash-tray in his bedroom, only a wicker basket. Before it occurred to him to use the wash-basin or the toilet for the ash and flame, he would open the window and flick them on the slates or thrust them into any antique vase or plant he could find.

Sometimes he also wore extravagant clothes, such as for instance a plaid or a multicoloured suit. If he had to use a microphone he would begin by kissing it with religious fervour after first wiping it with a handkerchief. He would explain the figures of speech in his poems at enormous length. At times his voice would rise to a manic shout and then sink to an impenetrable whisper. He would also tell the audience how the poem had been created and even read alternative versions of it. At times he would laugh bitterly, as if a poem was the record of a secret wound on which he did not wish to elaborate.

'Love,' he would say, 'What is love? It is a lethal cocktail. Our skin feels it but our hearts — no.' Or, 'Beauty, what can one say about it? All we have to do is consider Dostoievsky or Pascal.' He used such techniques with mainly rural audiences. With sophisticated audiences he would use pauses and silences: or he would stop in the middle of a poem. Or he might even leave the stage and come back later, his eyes apparently red from weeping.

If when he arrived there was only a tiny audience since, as the organiser often explained, there were alternative attractions such as a sermon or a professor giving a lecture about stones, he would look stunned. Then he would say, 'Is it for this that I came? Is it for this that I woke at six o'clock this morning? Is it for this that lust illuminates our mortal flesh?' Then he would say, 'Yes, it is indeed for this.' The organiser would feel so guilty that she would take him for a meal in an Indian restaurant, though she had originally intended to give him fish and chips.

In the restaurant, he would mutter over and over, 'The mysterious East. Have you read the immortal epic of Kalyani or indeed the fine miniature stories of Krishnabutari, so tiny that they could be written on the head of a gramophone needle?' He always refused rice, saying that it gave him heartburn. 'Do they not have bacon and eggs?' he would say, staring up at the ceiling adorned with mysterious drawings. 'Why do they not have pictures of Highland soldiers dressed in the tartan?' he would ask. If he was taken to an Italian restaurant he would mutter, 'I thought I would have been given some hard ecus in my change. Where are they?' And he would brood angrily for the rest of the night.

He had created also a long poem which was written in the Pictish language, and which was written on blue paper. 'Though we have little of that language,' he said, 'it is enough. Words such as "entrok" for "twilight", and "oberton" for "chariot" are inherently beautiful. And what can one say about "hok" which means the scent of hay on an autumn evening. I have loved this language since I saw my first inscription on one of its stones: "Orag rig dum", it read. It means "In fond memory of the sheep shearer Dum."'

His readings from his Pictish manuscript were received in respectful silence. He fielded all questions with avid aplomb. On these occasions he wore a long cloak fastened with a silver brooch. He told his audience of many Pictish customs, such as the Ingok and the Yor. Pictish poets, he said, had such respect for words that they spoke only in an inaudible monotone.

His poetry readings became more and more numerous. He travelled to France, Germany, the Philippines and Japan. 'What they say about geishas is not true,' he would say, but would not elaborate. An American scholar who had been listening to his Pictish poem said that Murdo had a primitive ferocity and at the same time calmness: an issue of a famous American magazine was devoted to the poem. He insisted on inserting footnotes which were sometimes three pages long. Young students adored his manic intensity. When it suited him he pretended not to have heard of Pound or Eliot, or said that they had not gone far enough. 'Poetry is infected by the germs of criticism,' he would say. Or, 'No genuine poet knows what his adjectives mean.'

And then quite suddenly he stopped attending poetry readings at all. 'I find,' he said, 'that after them I feel sordid and commonplace. I feel that audiences are coming to hear the poetry and not to see me. They, however, feel inadequate when confronted with me in the flesh and this in turn makes me feel guilty. How should I have this gift, I ask myself, when clearly they have none. Their faces shine with anticipation and ignorance. I am the high priest of their imagination. How disappointed I am when I see them. Furthermore, their questions are often impertinent or ambiguous. They ask for meaning when they should be seeking for magic. Poetry is hostile to church halls, I tell them.

'Also, I wish they would call me by my proper name when they introduce me. Did people make errors with Homer, Horace or Lucretius? Were there many alternative events when Dante was giving a reading? Was Virgil taken to an Indian restaurant?

'No, from now on I shall retain a holy silence. It is no use writing to me: I shall not answer. For poets to be authentic they must remain invisible. A stench arises from poetry readings when there should be incense. Statues do not walk in the daylight, legends do not parade about at night. The afflatus is not to be quenched by sherry or coffee. The door-keeper also dies and the organiser is as grass. The Arts Council will not suffer the torments of the desert. Mutability is all.'

And thus he would shoulder his spade and repair to the byre, where he would commune with the cows. 'Their liquid warmth fascinates me, their wavering outlines comfort me: and I also take the scythe to the hitherto upright corn. Life is not to be found in the city but here in the certainty of grass and hay. I have seen to the heart of things and I find it in the solitary and humble yet arrogant and gregarious lyric. We all suffer. I am tired of beer mats, microphones. I am exhausted by bardic hieroglyphics, errant posters no longer attract, nor am I enchanted by aseptic bedrooms where I am not allowed to smoke. Excuses will no longer satisfy. I shall reach the absolute logic of the poetry reading. I shall read to myself in the absolute holiness of mirrors. Janitors may glare at me, trains may be delayed, I shall return to the incorruptible legends of childhood. I have suffered. I was there.'

The byre appealed to him, with its authentic smell (the poetry of John Dung he called it): smoke rose from chimneys, an old woman, scythe on shoulder, chattered lightly to another. 'This is the dialectic of the ultimate sonnet.'

Last Will & Testament
by Murdo Macrae

1. To my beloved wife I leave my shoes
    and clothes, my pencil and my pen and
    my papers (all my love such as it is).

2. To my mother-in-law I leave
    the newspapers that I've been collecting
    for many years. And my red rubber
    nose.

3. To my father-in-law I leave a stone.

4. To tell the truth I haven't much else
    except my bicycle and I leave that also
    to my mother-in-law. And I leave my
    watch to Maxwell.

I wish my wife to send to following letter
through the post:

To Whomsoever it may Concern,

If anyone can tell me why we are alive, I will give him TWO POUNDS, all my own money.

For in the first place we are created of flesh and lightning.

And in the fullness of time the lightning and the flesh grow old.

And also we are working in a world without meaning.

Yesterday I looked at an egg and I couldn't understand why it was in the place that it was.

Now I should know the reason for its position in space. For that surely is not a mysterious thing. And I could say the same about butter. And salt. And Bovril. Now we have come out of the lightning, in our ragged clothes. And at last we arrived at Maxwell and his umbrella.

This is the problem that Newton never unravelled.

We kill each other.

For no reason at all.

These thoughts climb my head as if it were a staircase.

And that is why I am an idiot.

WE CANNOT LIVE WITHOUT SOME BELIEF.

I believe in my mother-in-law. She will live forever. She will be knitting in a country unknown to the Greeks.

I believe in my mother-in-law and my father-in-law and also in Mrs Macleod.

They will live forever.

For in their condition they are close to that of the animal.

They survive on dressers and sideboards.

Those who approach most closely to the condition of the animal are the ones most likely to survive.

And Woolworths.

Woolworths will live forever.

Too much intelligence is not good for one.

Too much of the spirit is not good for the body, but the following are good for the body:

BOVRIL, SANATOGEN, BUTTER, CROWDIE, EGGS, WATER, BREAD, MEAT.

And the sun on a warm day.

And a girl's breast,

and

a spoonful of honey.

I am sending you this letter, nameless one, with much happiness and without a stamp.

Murdo Macrae

ANTHEM

Avaunt, prognathous orators,
you spurious sports depart
we wish no smooth imperators
nor marble of the heart!

But come you leafy viators,
green stems of worth, upstart!
And a lack of hard proprietors
be "Ios" of our arts!!

Murdo's Business Letter

Dear Sir,

Hopeful of these things, I now conclude my letter to you. May they come, as we both ardently wish, I am sure, in the near future. We have worked long and hard for this, and have finally found the requisite equipment.

So I raise my glass to you, at this midnight hour, in the firm expectation that no efforts have been spared and the dwarfs of bureaucracy have finally been overthrown.

I have enjoyed working with you, as I hope you with me. And I hope the opportunity will arise again in the near future.

The prince, if I may so put it, has found the slipper, but the ball is still in our court.

> *Yours sincerely,*
> *and with kindest regards to your family,*
> *Murdo Macrae*

Enc.

Copies to: Mr Sprockett

                    Mr Burns-Nightingale

                    Mrs Tight Corset

                    Ms Sherry-Spiller

Murdo & His Future Readers

O future readers of my monologues, letters, remarks, jottings, I now say farewell to you. It may be that in your time, the DHSS will no longer exist, and writers like myself will breathe a natural and unrestricted air. In your days perhaps no one will be working at all, and there will be no more banks, car factories, fish farmers, etc. People will earn their bread by pressing the buttons of a computer, sitting in their own homes at their own desks. Such is the unsponsored dream that I have.

In those days I imagine the arts will flourish and Mrs Macleod will be able to rest and read Dostoievsky without having to listen to the seething of a pan on her kitchen stove.

Robots (from Japan perhaps) will in their infinite patience assume the drudgery of the masses and switch on and off the television for us. We will lie on sofas meditating on the infinite permutations of the universe while no low-flying jet will practise its gyrations overhead.

In those days there will be no wars, for men will become so sensitive that they will find it unthinkable to harm another human being except for certain games masters on the television.

There will be many poems, paintings, operas, unsolicited manuscripts, woollen pullovers, various kinds of bakery, jams, etc, etc.

There will be a computer of unimaginable proportions such that men and women will be able to do the leisurely work to which they are suited. Nor will they sweat and plot and suffer ignominy and sleepless nights in order to be chiefs and principals of this or that industry, whose aims are not theirs and whose working they do not understand.

In those days I prophesy unto you that the lion will lie down with the koala bear, and the tiger with the warthog. A new song will come to the lips of many, and they will no longer say, 'I am no gossip, but I am sure that Linda Morrison's skirt is too short.' On the contrary they will discuss the subtleties of structuralism and the meaning of the word 'precisely'. It is possible that an Irony Board may be created.

Minor poets, however, will say as before, 'Now I wish you to be quite brutal about my work, though I have sunk all my hopes in it,' and the honesty of reviews will vary with the distance of the reviewer from the reviewed, for human nature cannot be changed overnight.

Nevertheless, I am sure that men will progress and that you, distant reader, will look upon my amateurish anarchic jottings as the *cris de coeur* of one who was searching for a 'newer world', open, free, and generous, and you will say, 'He was a good man, not comical withal, but his heart was in the right place,' though I hope that you will not talk precisely in these terms but rather with a speech of infinite gradation, such that for instance you might have one word for 'one who though stupefied by boredom continues to smile while holding a glass of sherry in his hand,' (I suggest a 'cromp'), or 'one who speechifies at great length while the audience is seething with anger and rancour' (I suggest a smilebrog).

In any case I send my kindest regards to you, across the foam, jungle, veldt, etc, etc, O you men and women of the future, honest, open, lively, alert, and not hypocritical, free of bitterness or egotism, lovers of the arts, and in no sense mean, cruel or intolerant.

To you, my impossible readers, a fond farewell.
Murdo.

THOUGHTS OF
MURDO